The Thing

Johab stared, amazed, at the thing that came rumbling through the gates in the southern wall.

His father had told him of many of the things the Oldest of the Lords had made, back in the Mad Times. There had been machineries that removed the necessity for labor, making their people begin to lose their strength and capacities. Weapons too terrible for thinking upon, which poisoned the lands whereon they were used.

The Oldest of the Lords had been like children then, enchanted by the things that could be made with hands, oblivious to the greater potencies of mind and will. Of all their inventions, Johab had seen only the Triple Moons they had set into the skies of Rehannoth.

Until now . . .

Ace Science Fiction and Fantasy Books by Ardath Mayhar

ARDATH MAYHAR

LORDS OF THE TRIPLE MOONS

ACE SCIENCE FICTION BOOKS
NEW YORK

To Helen...
who likes my worlds

This Ace Science Fiction Book contains the complete
text of the original hardcover edition.

LORDS OF THE TRIPLE MOONS

An Ace Science Fiction Book / published by arrangement with
Atheneum

PRINTING HISTORY
Atheneum edition / 1983
Ace edition / May 1984

ISBN: 0-441-49246-0

Ace Science Fiction Books are published by The Berkley Publishing Group,
200 Madison Avenue, New York, New York 10016.
PRINTED IN THE UNITED STATES OF AMERICA

1

The Captive Child

Johab could feel a warm trickle down his side. The blood was already sticky, and his torn blouse tugged at the wound when he moved in the grip of the two men. They half-carried him down the curving flight of stairs, up which he had fled so short a time before.

The wide doors of the dining hall gaped open, broken from their hinges by the unexpected assault that had caught the family of the Lord Jolan at their evening meal. Johab's father still lay in his chair, his steely eyes open and surprised, the shaft that had pierced him still standing out from his wide chest. The boy looked once, then turned his eyes away. He did not even glance at the spot where his mother lay in a tumble of those she had killed before dying.

The rebels pulled him past the dining hall, toward the Chamber of Speech. Johab noted with grim satisfaction that one of them was dabbing at the stab wound in his upper arm. If he had only had a longer blade, he would have killed the man, he felt certain. But his father had said that not until he was ten could he habitually carry a sword. Only a short time, now, and he would be ten—but there would be, he knew quite well, no sword. In all probability there would be no tenth birthday, either, for he expected to die within minutes.

The Chamber of Speech was untouched by the sudden devastation that had visited the House of Enthala. In the tall chair where the Lords of this house had sat to hear complaint and to dispense aid and justice sat Golath, who had been a trusted under-steward for almost as long as the boy could remember.

Looking up into that fair face, with its daintily-trimmed blond beard, Johab felt his own expression freeze into something that sat strangely upon it. A chill hardness seemed to fill his small body, to reach its fingers even into his mind.

Golath sat gazing down at him for a long while, a slight smile on his face. Johab paid little heed to this scrutiny, for his inwardness was rearranging itself into another thing than that which it had been for his almost-ten years. One thought pulsed inside him, riding the flood of newness.

"You will pay for this, unfaithful steward. My father and my mother are past avenging this betrayal, and I can see in your eyes that you discount me as one who is years from reaching the maturity that will free the Gifts of the Old Lords. But if you are so stupid that you allow me to live, I shall bring you down into the dust of Rehannoth. Yes, and all those ragtag city folk who have allowed you to persuade them from the path of good sense." The words filled the room, unspoken though they were. Golath shifted uneasily and looked about as if for some threat. Johab felt a terrible smile bloom within himself.

"You are my prisoner," the man said at last. "I have saved you from my companions, though they would gladly have killed you along with the rest of your arrogant kind. But I know that the Lords hold power. I know that your training began the day you were born and that you will grow into one who can control strange matters and do unexplainable deeds. I will learn from you. I will take from you the secrets of the Old Lords. Fear me, Johab, for I hold your life in my hands."

The child said nothing. His golden-tan face was impassive,

his chilled-steel eyes steady. The smile inside him did not find its way to his lips. That would be premature—and dangerous. There would be time. If Golath intended to learn from him the ways of the Lords, there would be years and years of time.

Golath straightened in the crimson-cushioned chair. His eyes narrowed, and he said, "Look your last upon Enthala. We will pull it down before we return to my city. Nothing will be left in the Place of Juthar except the wind and the rubble. And the City of the Plain is now the City of Golath. Peopled with those I found in the far hills and on the seacoast and even at the edges of the mountains. People who fear and mislike the Lords because they cannot understand them. Though, of course, there are no longer any to understand. Except for you."

A gesture brought the toughs to the boy's sides. Another caused them to lift him from his feet by the elbows, forcing a groan from him as the wound in his side opened again, and a new flood of warmth moved against his skin. This lasted only a short time, as they bore him out the doors of the house, into the wide enclosure that his forefathers had walled away from the blasts that shook the Place of Juthar.

He wasn't thinking of the pain, however. He was thinking of Golath's words. All his people were gone? Jornaval of Olanthe, that great bear of a man, loved by his mountain kindred? Eslor, away on the seacoast in his Tower that dreamed toward the stars his family had charted and studied for generations? Kantris in the nothern hills? And, of course, all their children with them? There had been so few, here in these latter days. His father had often spoken sadly of that.

"When Rehannoth was younger, we were many," he had said. "Ninety families dwelled in this continent that is our world's only land mass. Though we lived far apart, there was much interaction, for we communicated constantly, mind-to-mind. And then something changed, so my fathers have written. We had few children. Families died away altogether. It became lonely. So lonely that we taught the man-creatures that emerged from the swamps, gave them fire and the notion of shelter and provision for hard times. They are our companions, now, and most are strong of heart and covetous of wisdom."

"Father didn't know *how* covetous!" he muttered under his breath. Then he lost the thought and stared, amazed, at the thing that came rumbling through the gates in the southern wall.

A crawler! His father had told him of many of the things the Oldest of Lords had made, back in the Mad Times. There had been machineries that removed the necessity for labor, making their people begin to lose their strength and their capacities. Weapons too terrible for thinking upon, which poisoned the lands whereon they were used. The Oldest of Lords had been like children then, enchanted by the things that could be made with hands, oblivious to the greater potencies of mind and will. Of all their inventions, Johab had seen only the Triple Moons that they had set into the skies of Rehannoth. Until now.

The two men heaved the boy into a compartment at the back of the mechanism. He hit in a twist, and darkness fell upon him in a rush.

2

A Locking of Wills

IT was days before Johab came to himself enough to think clearly again. Fever from his wound bore him away into strange countries of the spirit, where he thought that his mother and father visited him more than once. They talked with him earnestly, but he was never afterward able to remember what it was that they had said.

He was cared for by an old woman who washed his face with cold water and put cups of broth to his lips at times. She had seemed sorrowful, but the few times that he had tried to talk with her, to question her, she had touched her lips with trembling fingers and looked fearfully toward the door. He had understood, at last. Spies beyond the door. Perhaps listeners within the walls. He had noted several unlikely burls in the wood that finished them.

So he gave up trying to learn from his nurse and concentrated on growing strong again. Even at so young an age, he had had years of training to reinforce his will, and he accomplished the task more quickly than the old woman liked. She kept shaking her head at him, making silent motions that held more threat than clarity. But he knew what was in store for him. His kind had, after all, been putting moons into the sky before Golath's ancestors had crawled from the slime. This time of recovery was deceptive, the child knew. Weakening to his purpose, perhaps. He wanted to come to grips with the principal terrors as soon as possible.

That time came very soon. One morning the old nurse was sent away, tears sliding down her wrinkled gray cheeks. Johab was pulled from his bed, hair tousled, and told to dress immediately. Then he had been hauled away down echoing metal corridors, into an ornate hall, through a carven doorway into the presence of Golath.

A Golath changed, subtly, even from the man he had been so short a time before. Power sat upon his face. He was plumper, subtly softer. His face was flushed, behind the blond beard, and his eyes were those of a man who fears.

The boy was placed before him. He waved a beringed hand, and the guard backed from the chamber. Then he stared, once again, at his small captive.

"And what have you to say?" asked the man. "You've had time to think things over, I am sure. Are you ready to co-operate with me and my . . . associate? In return for the information that you can give us, we will provide you with a life that anyone might envy. Ease, servants, as much gold as you need or want. The things that your mind holds are worth that much to us."

Johab said nothing. His square face expressionless, he looked back into the eyes that regarded him, and there was no sign that he had heard Golath's words. Only a quiver of something like a silver fish moved for an instant behind those steely eyes.

"There would be no betrayal in it. Your people are gone. Beyond harm, now, for good or ill. And you wouldn't even be giving us many things that we do not have already in our possession. You saw the crawler. We have many more. We found, you see, the storehouse where your blind ancestors locked away the things that would have given them utmost power. And your father never knew—nor did that big fool

Jornaval, or their kindred. They had removed those things from their consciousness, and it never occurred to them that one who lived in Jolan's house and kept his records might also look into his ancestral writings.

"We have a weapon, Johab, that would allow one to remove this city from the plain, leaving behind only a burned place and glassy residue. What think you of that?"

At last, the boy responded. "Our fathers had the good sense and the decency to see, when that thing came into being, that it was too terrible to use. Ever. If you are less wise, that is unfortunate. My people, as you say, are no longer at risk, but I have affection for the plainsfolk."

"Those vermin? I have never understood why your father let them run free upon the plain that was his by long right. Without taxing them or even requiring that they labor for him. We may well test that weapon upon those stiff-necked folk."

"It is a weapon," said the boy, "that may well sever the hand that wields it. So my father told me many times. We had not forgotten the Old Weapons, Golath. We had proscribed them. For our own sake, as well as for that of the younger race living about us."

"Ahhh! Now you have told me what I wanted to know. You do know of the weaponry of your people. You are trained in their techniques, as I well know from seeing you go away into the plain with your father and into the tower with your mother. You can tell us many things that we must know!"

Johab laughed. "I know nothing of the proscribed weapons," he said. "We remembered their existence, but we deliberately forgot anything beyond our reasons for banning them. As for the things my people do . . . did . . . those are things that one does with his mind and his body and his will, working all together. I doubt that you could learn, even if I were willing to teach. Which I am not."

Golath pinched his lip between his fingers. He sighed. Then he smiled.

"In time, Johab. In time. I have men who worked in the places where your people made their devices still in use. The technicians are wiser than any others left in this world. They can take wire and metal and glass and make wonderful things from them. My . . . associate . . . worked closely with those, southward in Olanthe. They knew that the Lords engaged in trickery to deceive the people, for they understood the making of the abreet and the lenses and the power-changers used by your kind. Men who work metal do not believe in such nonsense as matter moved by will."

The boy laughed suddenly. "Did you ever ask them, Golath, where they got the metal they spun into wire? The glass that they shaped into lenses? And could they tell you?"

The man looked blank for a moment.

"I thought not. The Lords provided those things, not with machinery or with labor, but with will. Will that squeezed ores from the stone of the mountains, fused sand into glass, separated the different metals and shaped them into ingots. Ask them, Golath. They will say that the things they needed . . . simply appeared."

"Nonsense! But you will change. You are only a child. Time will change you. My . . . questioners will change you. And if those do not, then the metal cells will."

"The metal cells?" The boy had never heard of such a thing.

"My prison. I am drawing up the plans now. In time, I will be able to break the most obdurate, by means of my metal cells."

Johab stared at the man. The concept of having a place set aside in which to imprison human beings was so foreign to anything he knew that it took some time for the atrociousness of such a thing to be absorbed into his mind.

"It may be necessary to kill a man, if he poses a danger," he quoted from a long-ago lessoning, "but to imprison him kills the soul, which death could set free to find another form."

Golath, in his turn, laughed aloud.

Johab was beset, suddenly, with a burning desire to go into the man's mind, to understand fully the things that drove him to such irrational behavior. Then he controlled himself. That was a thing forbidden to his kind from the earliest time of its association with the younger race. Though the Lords and their kin moved freely through the minds of their own, they were scrupulous about leaving the less talented ones free from invasion of their private thoughts and control of their actions.

He heard footsteps behind him. Hands seized his arms again, and he was marched away. Not back to the room he had left but to a grim cubicle with a pile of straw in one corner and two buckets in another. Hard hands flung him onto the strawpile, and the heavy door creaked shut, leaving only a narrow ribbon of light to enter the dark chamber through a slit at a man's eye-level.

The boy sank against the wall and closed his eyes. There was a need to rethink many of the things that had been articles of faith among his kind.

I must read these people, though they are not my own. That was the first thought in his mind. The old rules had been fitted to other circumstances. They had—the thought was sudden and bitter—probably caused his father's death, the destruction of all the Old Lords left in Rehannoth. If Jolan or his wife had kept watch upon the thoughts of those who served them, things would have been very different!

But courtesy had demanded otherwise, and the Lords were —had been—the most unsuspicious of beings. He knew that Jornaval and Eslor and Kantris, their spouses and their young ones, had lived by the same code as had his parents. A pity. The first lesson he must take from this terrible circumstance was this: He, Johab, must watch, must listen, must probe where he could, learn what he might. And he must exercise his body and his mind as he had been taught.

The child blinked away tears. It would be years before he

matured. Until such time as he achieved his growth, his mature strength, he must wait here, at the mercy of Golath. But that time would not be wasted. He could spend every moment in tensing muscles, so subtly that no watcher might know what he did, and in strengthening the techniques his parents had taught him.

How long had it been since he had been brought away from Enthala? He had no clear recollection of the time he had been ill, but it could not have been less than a week or more than two. In a few days, however it was, he would pass his tenth birthday, the first step in becoming an adult. After that, if only he could survive and continue to grow in the things he had been taught, it would be only six or seven years until he might expect to be able to use the full powers of a Lord. To escape. To escape. . . . He laid his head on his arms and closed his eyes.

He wondered how it would be in those metal cells. He felt that he would find that for himself, in time to come.

3

In the Metal Cells

STEPS clanged above, echoing through the honeycomb complex that formed Golath's prison. Johab lay in the darkness of his cell, his senses in abeyance, his mind and his will focused upon inward things. Only when the door-slot at the top of his own cubicle rasped open did he bring himself back from those inward places and send a flick of attention toward the guard who was flashing his lightglass into the area, checking to see that the prisoner was alive and behaving himself.

With the ease of long practice, Johab slipped his thought into the man's skull without disturbing the mind thus exposed. "Useless thing! Shine the light, check off the prisoner as alive or dead, go on to the next. What difference does it make, at all?" grumbled the dim wits.

The boy went deeper, into places where information was stored. Then his skin prickled with shock, and his eyes sprang open, to see the slot of light disappear as the door was closed.

"They have used the weapon!" he said aloud, hearing his own voice for the first time in months. Perhaps years? He no longer even tried to account for time.

He sat in one smooth motion, drawing the controlled breaths that kept his lungs strong, stretching himself upright to go through the prescribed exercises. Now he was secure in the welcome darkness. The darkness that Golath thought would drive him to frantic acceptance of his captor's demands. He thrust his hands high, pushed his feet against the floor. In that almost suspended state, he sent out his mind for the first time since realizing that that much of his adult power had come to him.

He felt his way through the jumble of thoughts that filled the great house that Golath had built. Servants, guards, technicians, craftsmen were going about their duties in a haze of excitement. The sensation was quite clear to the young man. He touched, for the briefest of instants, the thought of Golath himself, but some fastidious instinct had always held him from probing his father's betrayer. He felt, obscurely, that such contact might pollute his own mind and purposes.

What? What was the thing that filled the halls and chambers with a buzz of talk and a humming of thought? Johab allowed himself to sink deeply into a cleaning woman, who was polishing a table. For an instant he caught a glimpse of her leathery face in the shining wood as she bent over her work. Then he was too deep for outward seeing.

And there was his answer. Golath, that purblind man, had actually used the most terrible of the Oldest Lords' weapons against a group of the plainsfolk. Pain filled Johab, jerking him free from the woman's mind, back into his own flesh.

"What was done once will be done again," he said aloud. His voice rasped in his throat and sounded strange to his ears.

He remembered Golath's words, long ago. *"Those vermin? I have never understood why your father let them run free upon the plain . . ."* The usurper's intent, even then, must have been to destroy those tough and independent people.

Johab laid himself carefully upon his sleeping-slab. Closing his eyes (though the darkness made that a thing of discipline rather than use), he envisioned the spot that he had chosen, when the time came, for his reappearance in the freedom of the plain. He sensed the camping-spot. Smelled it. Saw the rock, the scrubby growth, the old circle of stones, burnt dark with generations of campfires. It was so real! So real . . . but he was not there. The time had not come.

He sighed softly. He knew that he had exercised the preliminary teachings more concentratedly than any of his kind had ever done before. In the time that his length had increased by a third, his weight almost doubled, the capacities of his mind had increased incredibly. Every word ever spoken to him by his father or his mother or their peers had returned to his conscious thought. He had examined each idea, every precept from all sides. The doubts and questions that his solitary state had brought to mind had only served to reinforce his ultimate conviction that he held within himself abilities that could save and serve whatever of his plainsfolk might survive. Even a lone Lord, as he must be when he was at last able to remove himself from his prison.

As long as he had still been honing his skills, time had moved smoothly. He had no manner of measuring days or months or years, but they had flowed together in a stream of focused effort. The passing of the years had been irrelevant and not painful.

Yet now there was nothing left to do but to wait. He felt himself capable of anything, possible or not. Yet his body would not dissolve from this place and coalesce in that other toward which he yearned so strongly. How long must it be? He could not know. His father had indicated that the abilities came upon a young man between the ages of sixteen and seventeen and upon a young woman somewhat earlier. Now there was nothing to do except to endure the waiting.

And, of course, to bring his stocky body to a peak of condition. That was the thing that saved his sanity. He ran for leagues, never moving from the one spot large enough for such activity. He stretched his muscles into every conceivable position and toughened them to whipcord strength.

A day would come, he knew, when he would go free. When it came, he would be ready.

4

Sunrise

JOHAB did not raise his head. Still, he felt the sun as it heaved its hot orange bulk above the horizon. Without looking, he could see the warm glow spreading across the familiar landscape of wood-patches and plain, the place he had chosen.

He knew the instant the light would touch him, though he did not look. He remained crouched against the stubby tooth of rock that hid him, as he sat on the hummock rising from the plain. Warmth touched his neck, his back, wrapped him in comfort, after the stone-chill of the night and the metal-chill of his last resting place. Those rays were reaching into the west, now. Danger would come from there—was coming, he had no doubt. But he did not look.

For a long time he kept his curly brown head on his arm, as his inner seeing watched the progress of the sunlight. Then he sighed, stretched, and wriggled, serpent-swift, to a cleft in the rocky outcrop. He gazed westward, his young face intent, his pale eyes too old for his beardless face.

At the edge of vision he could make out sparks of gold and scarlet that he recognized as the colors of Golath and his associate Mirreh. Duller gleams were the crawlers on which they rode. He recognized with horror the sullen glints that marked the position of that terrible weapon that his people's law had forbidden. So—Golath brought it against him, young and alone. What horrid fears must drive the man!

Johab sank upon the warming stone and drew a slow breath. He had known that his escape would set the warren of the city buzzing. It had surprised him more than a little, all those years, that Golath had chosen to keep him alive, even when it became obvious that nothing would be gained by it. Mirreh had protested . . . sometimes violently. Johab had picked that from the minds of the techs who had taken turns at questioning him. He had known, as had his coconspirator, that the plainsfolk still held to their loyalty to the Old Lords, whatever means their new rulers used against them. The most dreaded weapon of all had only hardened the resolve of those who remained. And even the dull-witted townsfolk retained awe for their former rulers. The Lords had not, they now saw, driven them like cattle but had treated them as men. Only in their new circumstances had they begun to see the truth of the thing that Golath had done to them in setting his yoke about their necks.

Johab laughed suddenly, harshly. Well might the usurpers fear him. Those long years they had provided for him—in the solitary darkness of the metal cells—had given him time and opportunity to sharpen himself into a blade that might well cut off their years of rule. On the day that his family had died, he had put off the softness of childhood, the trusting ways of one reared in love and courtesy. Now, sitting alone upon the rock, he was, he thought, far more dangerous and potent than he could have been, left in peace in his old life.

He again applied his eye to the cleft. The glints were now brighter, sharper. The armor-clad shapes were now discernible as men, bundled in the thick stuff that warded away the breath of the great weapon they followed. The crawling machines had acquired shape and detail. The angles of the weapon showed clearly.

So many men, so many crawlers, such a powerful weapon to recapture one lone prisoner who had escaped Golath's cells!

He laughed again, mirthlessly. He had only the robe he stood in, the dilapidated cloth sandals on his feet, and a crystal-studded ring of brass that clasped his upper arm. Golath had not removed it, for it seemed that in order to do so the arm itself must be cut off. Yet it had accommodated itself to his growth from seven to seventeen.

He had also himself: his short stocky frame, which he had hardened with exercise in the cells; and his mind, with its esoteric powers that had been trained while his father, the most talented of the Old Lords, lived, in the uses of the strange abilities his race possessed, and exercised to sharpness in the dark and quiet he had been given.

And there were his erstwhile captors, in their seeming strength, ramping across the plain, filled with wonder and anger and, no doubt, fear at his escape. None had ever before fled the metal cells. Yet those powers of the mind that he had polished so carefully in the unending night of his captivity had at last brought him out.

He looked about him again, at this spot he had chosen in that narrow darkness, a spot that had been a familiar haunt of his childhood. He had often camped here with his father in the days of his training. Lying quietly, he had let his senses persuade him that he was truly here. He had smelled the dusty sweetness of the plains air, the tang of the low-growing bushes in the rock clefts. He had seen the triple moons spinning on the horizon, the dizzy shifting of their light spattering the outcrop above his head. He had felt the pebbles grating beneath his shoulder blades. And it had become real.

The cell had faded like smoke on the wind, and he had been here, on this hillock, in the chill of midnight. Crouched in a huddle against the cold, he had reveled in the freedom of the night, until the rising sun had warmed him to action.

Now the sun was well up. Johab gauged its angle with calculation. He smiled. Given the proper conditions, a small gift of fortune from the hands of fate, he might yet make his mark upon the murderers of his father and his kin. Even now, his enemies had set themselves in the quarter of the compass that he would have chosen for them, given the chance.

He turned his face to the sun, half-closing his pale eyes against the now-fiery brilliance of its glare. That great star would fill a goodly fraction of the sky behind him, if his pursuers approached in good time. Its heat was even now making the rocks around him shimmer and waver. The line of approaching men seemed to dance above the earth of the plain as it came toward him.

Faster . . . they must come faster. He stood on the little hill, then he climbed to the top of the rock and folded his arms across his chest, gazing calmly across the distance that separated him from his foes. A flicker of movement nearer at hand caught his attention.

A mop of sun-bleached hair above a leather-tanned shoulder came suddenly into sight in one of the patches of woodland that dotted the plain. Johab started, tried to see with his physical eyes and could not. He closed them and sought with his inner seeing.

A band of roughly dressed and ill-armed men and women broke from the wood, keeping it between themselves and the approaching troops. Running desperately, they came near the hillock, passed around it, and gathered on the sunward side. They looked up at Johab, who now opened his eyes and stared down at them.

The owner of the pale hair stood forward. "You are the Lord Johab, long declared dead by the Lord Golath?" he asked, yet he did not truly question.

"I am," answered the man on the rock. "The Old Ones did not lie, then, when they said that the folk of the lost lands had talents that showed them, without fail, what passed upon their own lands."

"Not all of us, Lord," said the man. "Yet we have those who see afar and know that which will come to pass. For three days we have watched upon the plain for you. We are here to die with you, when those who follow you come to this place."

Johab's tight face softened. The sternness that had lived in his eyes for so long lightened. "Not yet, my children, has the time come for you to die," he said. "Though I am the last and the least of the Old Lords, I have some of their knowledge and skill. It may be that if those upon the way will come swiftly, before the sun is halfway up the sky, I may destroy them. Yet even if it is my time now to die, I would not take with me those who are the seed of the future. The townsfolk have little kidney for danger and are soft folk with lazy minds. Live, my children, for the day when the usurpers weaken. For they will weaken; be certain of it. Then do battle with them for the future of Rehannoth."

Johab spread his arms as if to embrace them; then he gestured toward the plain to the east. "Go swiftly back to your own places. Remember me and the Old Lords and the teachings that have made you free men for these many ages. Go!"

Upon his word, they went, though not with a good will. Some turned time and again, but he waved them on until the last disappeared into the sun-shimmer. Then he turned his face back to the west and felt the heat of the sun along his bloodstream and the warmth of spirit, which was the love of his people, in the marrow of his bones.

The growl of the crawlers was borne to him on the light breeze, with the clank of the armor and weapons. The line of men came swiftly, and now he could see the markings on their metal hoods and the bulky armor that protected them from the breath of the Forbidden Weapon. Johab touched the ring above his elbow, tracing its patterns with his finger, round thus, back thus, crosswise THUS. It opened into his hand.

Now he stood tall and reached for the top of the outcrop, swinging himself up. Raising the armband high, he turned the crystal setting toward the sun, focusing its light to a more-than-brilliant point on the soil at the hillock's foot. Then he faced the oncoming troop and sought out the shape of the weapon that had been brought against him.

"Against me . . . against ME, you fools, you bring the weapon made by my people ages before your own folk crawled from the swamplands! Wisdom you have never owned, but folly is your master! Go back to your beginnings!" he cried aloud, though he knew that none could hear him across the distance and above the noisy mechanisms.

Upon the great weapon he saw the patterns that had been etched by his long-fathers. He let them draw nearer until he could trace them in detail. Then he closed his eyes and drew upon his inner vision, moving his hand, holding the crystal so that it cast a far, tiny point of light upon those markings. That speck of light, too small for the men nearby to see, faithfully followed the intricacies of the patterns, tracing them round the convolutions and angles.

The weapon began to glow, faintly, then brighter. Johab saw and exulted, but his hand moved on as steadily as the sun that moved up behind him.

Then he heard a cry, still faint and far with distance. One among the troop, he knew, had seen the danger. He opened his eyes and looked full upon the line, which was falling into confusion. The great weapon was pulsing with fiery light, its patterns flashing into greater brilliance with each pulsation. Johab laughed. He felt his own laughter as the only cold thing in all the burning plain. Then he tumbled to his knees behind the rock.

There was a terrible blast of light that seemed to come through the stone of the hill. He felt the trees on the plain withering away to ash and the rocks flowing. He sent a thought outward toward his folk, but they were well away and safe. Then he felt westward toward his enemies. There was no life there.

He felt the patter of pebbles begin about him, and he knew that the time had come to go. Yet he delayed, kneeling in the dust of the hillock, long enough to shape, with stones too large for shifting in the winds, the symbol that was his own and that of the Old Lords.

"Let those who come to seek the seekers look long upon that," he said to the watching sun. "Johab is upon the lands, and they may seek him more warily in time to come."

Then he walked into the east, on the track of the people, and the sun cast his long shadow across the trembling plain.

5

Forenoon

The sun burned orange-red, mounting toward noon. On all the wide reaches of the plain that scorched beneath its rays, there was no sound save the continual patter of falling stones and clods of soil and the steps of Johab. He moved at times with eyes closed, seeking before him, and there was a grim smile upon his lips.

Behind him towered a terrible column of smoke, mixed with the stuff of the plain and the atoms of the troop that had come after him. But he turned no part of his attention to the west. Golath could wait, with his fellow-traitor Mirreh, upon the pleasure of Johab, last of the Old Lords and, perhaps, first of the New.

Now he must find the people of the plain and teach them the arts that his own kind had taught to him, to be preserved in human memory, whether he lived or perished. And those arts might well insure freedom for those whom he taught.

His feet crunched steadily over the brittle grass and the mica-starred grit of the plain. He knew when he passed each clump of trees, for there was always a many-faceted stirring of life-sparks within his inner-seeing that told of the presence of small beasts, sheltering there from the growing blaze of sunlight. They were faint and soon gone, but the strong impulse that was the trace of a village of plainsfolk burned before him with all the intensity of the sun itself.

He opened his eyes and trudged on, ignoring the faint rain of grit, which was now all that fell from the sky. The pinkish soil glowed in the warm light that was only faintly dimmed by the dust in the sky. He smiled. Again he was free upon the lands of his people! The shadows of the copses, the very shapes of the stones were pleasure to his eyes.

He approached another of the rounded wood-patches now, noting the sturdy growth of leatherwood domed above the tangle of merryberry and dallbush. His soles were burning through the thin prison sandals he wore, and he coveted thicker foot covering.

Slipping through the undergrowth, he found the bole of a tree of suitable girth and ran his eye up its length. With a start, he recognized the shape of an abreet perched upon a limb beneath the parasol-shaped crown. Abruptly he sat down amid the herbage and concentrated on the thing. Within it . . . yes, within it was still potential. He could feel the waiting of its energy, untapped these many years. Its bird-shape seemed unimpaired. When the last of the Towers of his folk had fallen, when the last of the controlling minds had died, it must have sunk to rest here with whatever residue of energy remained within it. It had waited, with mechanical faithfulness, for his need. Now he had eyes that might range far without draining his energies: a weapon that any foe might wisely fear.

Johab stood again. The abreet would wait now while he tended his sore feet. He felt the tree trunk with a probing finger. Just here, he thought, was the edge of a section of bark. With his nails he worried at it, loosening a side, another, then peeling a large flap away. Again he sat, laying the flexible sheet in his lap, feeling in the cool dimness for the layerings at its edge. A tough sheet peeled off with a hissing sound, then another.

Swift work with a merryberry thorn and ravelings from his loose robe created a pair of lapped boots, which he drew on over his sandals. Flexing his toes, he delighted in the cool comfort of his new footgear.

Now for the abreet. He leaned against the tree and again traced the pattern that loosed the crystal and his bracelet. It dropped into his hand, winking as though it gathered into itself every ray of light in the shadowy wood. Johab held it out into a ray of sun that slipped through a rent in the foliage above. The crystal shimmered almost angrily. A thrill of energy-potential hummed up his arm, and he hastily moved the stone, turning it so that its strange facets directed the refracted ray into the treetop, bathing the abreet in its light.

There was a sound from the treetop. Not quite a chirp; not quite a hum or a purr. A *breeerp* sort of sound. Johab felt tears rise behind his eyes. His own abreet, given him as a toddler, had been a part of his life. The sound from the tree brought back to him the games, the hunts, the joyful days of his boyhood, and it brought back also faces long cold in their graves —if graves they had had at all. It sent rising before his eyes the long years of harmonious rule, the love of his father for his folk, and the final treachery that had brought all to dust and himself beneath the heel of Golath.

But now the abreet was moving, stretching its stubby wings with a metallic rustle, rising upon its three-toed feet. In its dormant huddle, it had seemed very birdlike, but now he could see its distinctive shape against the leafy background. The dark sheen of its metal glinted in the ray, and its body, too rounded for the size of the wings, reflected sparks of light. Seen thus, it was a device. When it soared high, seeing with its powered eye-cells, none upon the ground would suspect that it was no carrion-bird, circling. And its sun-powered energies drew nothing from the mind that directed it. Johab sighed. Well enough, for his own energies were waning with weariness and lack of food.

He signaled the thing above. The abreet soared from the treetop and began riding an air current into the upper reaches of the sky. He closed his eyes and allowed his mind to see through its cells. To the west a pall of dust still hung over the land. Beyond . . . far beyond . . . he could glimpse the roll of hills that held the hold of Golath.

The abreet circled. To the east, the plain stretched below in wood-dappled undulations, marked only by the outcrops of stone that crowned hillocks similar to that on which he had stood.

Upon the plain, people were moving, and he knew them to be those who had sought to aid him. They were moving more swiftly than seemed possible for folk afoot in the blazing heat, but Johab knew the rigor of their lives and training and the determination of their spirits. They would move so for him because he had ordered it. They would do it for love of the Lords before him, for they had dealt justly with the people of the plains down the long ages. But none might ever hope to drive them, even at a walk.

Sight veered southward. There, mountains marched at the very edge of vision, mountains dark with a furring of forests. There lay the lair of Mirreh. Beyond were the scattered holdings and eyries of the mountain folk.

Johab urged the abreet higher. He felt a compulsion in the south. The mountains lay upon the horizon like shaggy beasts waiting for prey. Something stirred there, but no sign of it could be seen by the powerful eyes of the device. Johab sighed in his forsaken body and turned his creature northward.

There the plain went on as if unending. Men afoot, he knew, could travel for a hundred sun-spans before reaching the hills that edged it. Beyond the leagues of hills lay the troubled reaches of the ocean. And beyond the ocean lay only ocean still, until the planet rounded again to the other side of its vast and lonely continent.

So. Nothing moved within his boundaries save that which belonged there. Danger, perhaps, to the south. Nothing to the north that was discernible to his senses. The south and the west were the fountainheads of peril. He called to the abreet's mind-centers, and the device came down to sit again upon the branch where it had spent so many years.

Johab, mindful of his depleted energies, munched a handful of dry merryberries, savoring their sweet-tart flavor but badly craving moisture. He burrowed under a nearby dallbush, searching, and was rewarded by a glimpse of three-lobed leaves and a bulbous stem. He carefully snapped off the upper part of the stem, leaving enough of the plant to flower and reproduce. Chewing on the sour-juicy pulp, he lay back and gazed into the dome of living green above him. After all the imprisoned years, he was again free.

Sleep overtook him in the wood-shadow. He slept as he had forgotten how to do in the tension-ridden years of his captivity. Once again an abreet kept watch above him; once again the dry-sweet air of the plains soothed him, and the penetrating heat of the sun comforted his flesh. Sleep was restoration of power, regeneration of mind and body and heart.

On its high perch, the abreet purred. Its eye-cells swiveled, noting anything that moved on the plains.

Johab woke to peace of heart. Sun-darts danced across him as the high-layered leaves swayed in the wind. He could see that the light came to him from near the sun's zenith. He sighed and stretched, coming erect in the same breath.

"Come!" he called to the abreet, knowing well that his thought was sufficient to compel it, but enjoying the sound of his own voice after so many voiceless years.

He moved from shadow into the full fury of noon sun. As hammer on glowing metal, it smote the land. Even Johab, plains-son that he was, almost expected to feel molten sand lap about his feet. He smiled grimly, fiercely. No soft soldier of Golath could ever follow plainsfolk under the midday sun.

Only when the evening shades had cooled the countryside might the townsmen venture upon the open lands.

The usurpers might preen in towns built by those stronger and wiser than they. They might claim overlordship of those with little spine. But they well knew that their writ did not run in the wild lands, that their dominion did not extend to the powers allied to sun and moons that the Old Lords had held.

Now Johab walked swiftly, his eyes fixed on the horizon. He knew the abreet, from its vantage point in the sky, would relay to him knowledge of friend or enemy. His feet, secure in their new boots, slid deftly over sink-holes and crusted spots, the habits of his youth guiding them unerringly. As the sun rode over his head he felt an explosion of sensation behind his eyes. He was nearing his destination. The folk of the plains were about to see their Lord again.

6

Noontide

As Johab moved across the plain, and the abreet circled above, Johab had the wry notion to watch himself trudging across the inferno from that lofty station.

A strange sensation indeed! Here he strode in the crushing heat, the grit stirred by his boots grating in his throat. Yet here he hung in the sky, watching a tiny point of darkness on the dappled sun-mirror that was the plain.

The abreet wing-tilted, and its angle of vision changed. On the edge of the sky was a dim huddle of shapes that could only be the village of the people whom he followed. They had told him that some lived among them who possessed the powers of the mind. Abruptly, he deserted the abreet and closed his eyes, though his feet never interrupted their rhythm.

Now he hurled toward that distant village a bolt of thought/vision/feeling that held all the urgency he could muster. Lifting his arm, he turned the crystal in the bracelet so the full energy of the sun rayed through it. A jolt of power ran through him, and he increased the magnitude of his sending. Then he paused and waited for some signal that showed he had been heard.

He stood still in the terrible flood of sunlight, his shadow pooled at his feet in an inky puddle. All his senses were open, waiting for a reply. Then, at the edge of perception, there was a ripple of sensation that built, moment by moment, into a current of emotion that reached his waiting spirit as wonder/doubt/joy. Johab smiled.

His people were waiting.

He raised his arms in a gesture of victory, then he walked onward, the abreet circling silently above, toward the village. In mid-stride, he was jolted, staggered, almost felled by a mental cry of such power that it left him swaying on his feet, drained by its terrible potency.

"Help me!" it shouted in his mind. "Turn your thought to me . . . turn your thought to the south, to the mountains! Oh, hear me!"

Johab stood on the plain, his orientation disrupted by one overriding thought. "One of my people still lives!" he shouted up at the abreet. "One of my own kin still draws breath in the lands!"

Then he turned aside into a copse of leatherwood and sat against a cool bole, turning his mind southward. He recalled the contours of those distant mountains, with their dark forests and their taint of danger. His outward-seeking thought was seized as if it had been a straw in a whirlwind and sucked in one great swoop into the mind of that desperate seeker in the southlands.

He could see dimly the roughly cut stone walls that were aglimmer, here and there, with seeping moisture. The sound of its trickling was mixed with a distant murmur of voices and the rattle of metal against metal. His borrowed wrists told him the source of the sound, as he became aware of shackles. He hung by wrists and ankles against the slimy chill of the wall. For one heartbeat his host . . . no, by the triple moons! His hostess! . . . let into her consciousness the pain of those swollen and all-but-skinless members.

"I am Johab, Lord of the Plainsfolk," whispered his spirit to hers. "I have come from captivity, also, but none such as this. I dwelt for a long time as Golath's . . . guest. Yet he follows the old teachings and forswears torture as a means of subduing his captives."

"Would that Mirreh were so advanced," came the wry reply. "I am Ellora, daughter of the Lord Jornaval, who ruled the mountains to the southern coastline. It seems plain that I am the last of my blood left in the south. Otherwise, this barbarian would have had me killed long ago. Yet he still hopes to wrest from me the secrets of my fathers. It is my good fortune that his mind holds no place that is capable of comprehension of such powers of the mind and spirit as our people learned."

"None among the usurpers believe in them," Johab replied. "I probed the techs and the thinkers Golath sent to me. They are closed to our ways, but they are shrewd in their own. Else we would not now be the last of our people left in all Rehannoth.

"I was the captive of Golath for seven years. As I lay in darkness in his metal cells, I honed myself, sharpening all that I had learned of the ways of our people. At the last, I reached the age of maturity and was able to come free of my prison. I brought into being a place as familiar to me as my own chamber. When I opened my eyes, it was to see stars, moons whirling where our fathers set them in past ages. You should be able to do the same."

"Surely." Ellora's thought was grim. "But all places that I know well enough are occupied by Mirreh's henchmen. A girl-child is not encouraged to camp in the wild or to rove unsupervised. The first time I moved to a place that I knew well there were troops there, but they were fearful when I appeared before them. I was able to run for a day, and then the tattle of the folk brought new troops. And when the people realized that I was flesh and blood as were they, they lost their awe. Word went out into all the countryside that I might appear and must be recaptured and bound and taken back to Mirreh.

All my escapes led only to capture, for the places to which I had been taken often were those frequented by many people. I know no wild and isolated spots from which I can move unseen into yet safer places. Else I would not be here, you can be certain."

Johab thought deeply. "With two of the Old Lords to guide them, the people of the plain might become potent enough to hold their own against the usurpers," he said at last. "Surely we may find a way to free you."

A crunching of boots on gritty stone interrupted their thought. Light flickered more strongly, glancing from the wet stone and from bright flecks deep in the rock. It danced on the shackles that bound Ellora to the wall, as a torch was brought around the bend in the tunnel.

It was borne in a great fist corded with knots of muscle. The face behind the light was scarred and twisted as though by the touch of flame, and it assumed strange expressions as the torchlight moved upon it. But it was obvious that little mind dwelt behind those deep-set eyes, and less thought marked the brow. Johab knew that this was Mirreh's bodyguard. Indeed, that cautious man walked close behind his hulking attendant.

The torch was thrust high to shed light on the captive, and its rays also revealed the face of Mirreh. Long, narrow and pale, it was the face of a clerk or a merchant, Johab thought, holding no trace of the qualities befitting a Lord. His form was tall but slight, and he stood hunched, with his chin sunk into the cowl of his robe. Glints of gold, sparks of living fire from jewels danced in the torchlight from neck and wrists and waist, but they lent him none of their own vigor.

The colorless eyes narrowed, the mouth opened like the flat jaws of a trap. "So you are brought to this, Ellora. Chains and a dungeon are much less than I offered for your cooperation. You might have lived, still, in your old way, if you had listened to my counsel. Yet you cling to the past, to the ridiculous legends fostered by your people to overawe the common folk.

"You have escaped three times. So I know, beyond all doubting, that you still possess at least one of the devices the Old Lords made. None has denied that they were clever at such. It was only by use of devices that they kept all the lands subdued for so many ages. For the knowledge of such weapons we would give much . . ." his voice dwindled to a whisper, then to silence, and he stood hunched, gazing speculatively at the girl upon the wall.

She laughed, and the ring of real amusement was in her voice. "Truly, Mirreh, you are a man of consistent mind. My father judged you so, and so he told me. He said to beware of such, for they are incapable of learning anything new or strange. So I tell you again, I have no device at my command. My only weapons are my mind and my training. These are much, as you have learned without learning. There were devices, indeed, weapons of strength beyond imagining. My father destroyed all his weapons in the southern lands, with the last of his strength, when he knew that your rebellion must prevail. I can give you nothing except my contempt, and you have that already, in good measure."

The man's mouth turned downward in an ugly arc. His nostrils flared, then pinched close. "There is always death . . ." he began, but Ellora interrupted him with another laugh.

"When you set me free through death, you will receive the only blessing I will ever direct toward you. Know, Mirreh, that if I possessed even one of the least of my people's weapons I could, from this deep prison, destroy your precious city and leave your bones powdering in its dust. By this, you may reason, if such an ability is yours, that I would have done this already, if I could. Now go back to Olanthe. Walk upon its wall. Look into its streets, busy with the toil of your slaves. Wonder if I may not, in some way, hunt out a surviving device and dissolve your kingdom beneath you."

But the thin man had turned on his heel and hurried away

31

into the darkness, leaving his torch-bearer to follow in his wake.

Johab, many leagues away in his own body, was chuckling. "Do you always bait him thus?" he asked Ellora. "He has gone away convinced, more than ever he was, that you bear within your mind precious secrets that he must attain."

"So I do, Johab. There is one cache of weaponry that my father did not destroy, for it was not his. Your own father, Jolan, foresaw a time of need. He went among all the Lords, persuading them to make an armory containing one device of every kind that they had at their command. This they did, hiding the place in the mountains, under my father's rule.

"He told no one except the Lords themselves the location, and even to them he gave cryptic instructions. It was done long ago, before either of us was born, but he told me my own clue. He said that it would fit, as key in lock, with that of any of the other Lords. I have found no trace in all the mountains of any such store. Still, I possess a key with no lock. Might it be that you have a lock with no key?"

Johab searched through all his memories of his father's admonitions, but no hint came to mind. "All was lost suddenly in our lands, through the treachery of Golath, who was our steward. My father was the first to die, for our gates were opened secretly, and hordes of the enemy poured in upon us. He was stricken to the heart with a bolt before we knew they were there. It may be that he had waited until I reached maturity to tell me, and there was no time before he died."

Ellora brought forth from the deeps of her mind a thought. Johab shuddered at its shape. "There is a way," she said. "Were you not taught, before the end of things, the ways for reaching the minds of the dead?"

"Aye," came Johab's answering thought, as a pale whisper. "Never did I think to use it. My father, at rest in the Lands Beyond, I had thought to leave to his repose at the feet of the gods. Yet I must find him and take the secret, for my heart tells me that the usurpers are not yet to know ease in their stolen realms."

"Go, then, back to your own place," commanded Ellora. "You need have no fear of finding me again. I seldom go abroad, and I never travel."

Again Johab chuckled. "It troubles my heart to leave you here," he said. "But you have your beasts to bait for amusement, until I return."

Then there was a moment of blank and whirling darkness, and he found himself totally beneath the leatherwood, stiff in his limbs but beginning to feel the stirring of hopefulness in his spirit.

7

Beyond Midnight

JOHAB stood beneath a sky that shone like polished ebonstone. He could see the dark sweep of the plain that lay to the south. Above the village, the triple moons spun madly, making the youth's shadows whirl at his feet in complex dances. About him, the village lay sleeping, exhausted by an evening of such celebration as the folk of the plains had never thought to know again.

The Old Ones slept now, worn with the unaccustomed excitement of his arrival, as well as with preparations for fulfilling the strange request he had made of them. Their hands twitched and their feet moved as they slept. Their faces wrinkled with dim dread, as their dreams recalled to them their linkage with Johab. They were draining their energies and their talents into his, even while they dreamed of the obscure and terrifying purpose that called forth his need. None of the elders lay peacefully in their beds, for the shadow of their young Lord's intention was upon their spirits, sending them into the deep, dark places of the heart.

Now Johab stood alone before the smooth-rounded house of clay that had been given him. He looked deeply into the sky, beseechingly toward the south, hopefully at the triple moons. He loosed his bracelet yet again and held it above him, focusing upon his face the concentrated kaleidoscope of light that played through the crystal. He could almost feel the patterns move upon his skin. His hair stirred with electric current, and he could feel the potential building within him. He lowered the bracelet, set it again about his arm, then turned toward his house.

The darkness within hindered him not at all. He had been for so long in the darkness of his prison that it seemed almost more natural to him than light. He moved to his couch, knelt on the matting beside it to touch his forehead to the floor, and said, "Let all be done according to the purposes of the gods. If this that I seek to do is ill-done in Your eyes, let me perish in the doing." Then he lay upon his bed and closed his eyes.

There was a deeper darkness than any before. It filled his skull; his ears and nostrils seemed stopped with its black thicknesses. He pulled away from himself, leaving the still form that was himself to lie in that miasma. He went out, but no plain bathed in starlight and moonlight fled beneath him, only swirling mists of night hues. He fled through the mists, blind, yet knowing direction and destination without understanding how he knew.

"Father," his spirit whispered. "Father!"

Now there was cold, though he had no flesh to feel it. Colder than anything that life could know was the place through which he moved. Fear crouched beneath the mists, waiting for him to falter in his purpose. But the years in the metal cells had armed him against hesitancy and doubt. He sped onward, moving toward something that gave an answer to his calling, a faint spark of warmth in the deadly chill. An entity was there that was bound to him in spirit and must answer his cry, even from the place of death.

With vision that had no eyes, he saw before him, thrusting lightning-colored shapes through the mists, a chain of mountains. Above them rippled banners of color more vivid than any aurora. About their sides played storms of crimson fire. He approached those slopes with dread and ardor, and his winging spirit rose high above their coruscating surfaces until he could see over the highest ridge into the valley beyond.

The brightness of the valley dimmed the brightness of the mountains to candle-paleness. He forgot the storms that burned beneath him, the sharp spires of power-charged peaks that reached for him as he passed. He saw only the glow of the place at the feet of the gods, where he might find his father's spirit. He set his heart to reach it.

But there came a point beyond which he could not move. As a wall of glass, it hung invisible between him and his goal. His mind-self fluttered against it, seeking, seeking, but there was no way to enter. Then he settled down until he touched grassy meadow with his shadow-feet, and the ghosts of tears ran down his intangible cheeks.

"Father!" he cried once more. "There is a thing that I must know!"

For a long while there was no answer. He sat on a stone, though no weight of flesh bore upon him, and looked about his feet. A thousand yellow flowers bloomed amid the meadow grasses, spreading their flat, many-petaled faces upward, as if to comfort him. Though there was no sun, the place where he waited was bright with golden light, and a butterfly of ice hue, sprinkled with rubies, whirled above the blossoms. Nearer it came, settling now upon one, now upon another of the blooms, until it lit at last upon his hand.

The hand grew warm, as though it were held in that of his sire in days long ago. A small voice said, "My son, what brings you, before your time, into the lands of those who have done with life?"

Johab held his hand very still and gazed in awe at that jeweled creature upon it. It raised and lowered its wings, as though showing off their delicate loveliness, turning about so that he might admire it from all sides.

"Many fearful things I have heard and thought of the place

beyond death, my father," he said at last, "but little did I think to find you in such a form, amid such beauty."

"For as long as I wish, I may do the slight work of such as this, Johab. I may exist in utter purity of spirit and beauty of form, without burden, even of procreation. Such is the way of things here. When my spirit is healed of the wounds of living, refreshed and anxious to go forth again and do the arduous tasks, it will be set into a proper shape and given a work that is fitting.

"But tell me your need, for I may not remain with you over-long, and you must return through the mists soon, or they will close, trackless, and your body will know you no more."

So Johab told his father of his need and his mission, of Ellora and the weapons cache and their plan. The butterfly crouched on its spun-glass legs, its faceted eyes glinting in the unearthly light, listening. When he had done, it stood and stretched its wings.

"Such little things . . . it seems long since I dealt with little things. But the key you need is this: *The Chasm of Genlith, to the right.* Fit this with Ellora's words, and you will find and open the storehouse. Know, my son, that the mists will wash away all remembrance of this place, of me, and of what I have told you. But when you gaze again upon the triple moons, you will recall the key, word for word, as I have given it to you. Farewell. It will be some time before we meet, but for me it will be tomorrow. Go in strength and peace of heart. Go in the ways of the gods."

The butterfly lifted its wings once, twice, was airborne, and was gone.

Johab stood motionless, for a time, stricken to the heart with wonder. Then he turned his spirit toward the mists and set out for his distant body, which called to him with all the warm linkage of life and flesh.

When his eyes opened, the darkness had thinned. Starlight blazed through the unshuttered windows. He blinked, stretched and sat, unable for a time to orient himself. Then he stood and went to the door, looking toward the horizon where the triple moons hung just above the curve of the plain. Into his mind crept the words, "The Chasm of Genlith, to the right."

Johab dropped to his knees and hid his face in his hands. "I have gone into the lands beyond death and come forth again, and I cannot remember! Yet the words are within me, and the weapons of our fathers are within our grasp."

He turned to his house and lay upon his bed, to sleep until the sun was high and the plain ashimmer with the heat of its blaze.

The purring *"Breeerp!"* of the abreet woke Johab from his sleep, bringing him to his feet. At the door of his house stood the eldest of the Old Ones, his face anxious and worn, his hands burdened with two large bowls, which steamed, even in the growing heat of the forenoon.

"Clan-Father, you need not weary yourself in my service!" said the youth, taking the food from his hands. "Come into my house and sit with me as I eat. I have many questions that need answering." He led the old man into the house and saw him seated. Then he sat himself upon the bed and began to eat.

"Lord," the Old One quavered, "our fear was great, in the night. It has been long and long and longer still since any we knew dared the paths of the dead. The oldest of us can remember only two of the Lords who ventured thus, calling upon our strengths for aid. One returned. One did not. Our sadness would have been deeper than ever before, if we had come to you today and found your flesh untenanted."

"I journeyed far in the night, but no memory of it remains with me," said Johab, setting aside his bowls and cleansing his hands and face upon a cloth. "Yet I returned with the answer that I sought. So it is that I know that somewhere in the darkness of the place of death I did indeed find my father and spoke with him. He gave me a key to aid us all in unlocking the shackles the usurpers seek to set upon us. Are the folk of the plains content? Or do they seek a new road, a new goal for themselves and their children after them?"

The Old One drew himself up in the chair, straightening his bent back. "Lord, no child of the plains has yet bent his neck to the yoke of the usurpers. No traitor has appeared among our number to sell us into slavery. Our pride, which we have always had through working with your own kind, is all that we possess. We had thought to live out what days are left to us with only pride and memories—and freedom. If you can show us work fit for a free people, we will follow you, though it cost the last drop of our blood, the last breath of the last babe.

"The new lords of the lands are determined to destroy all who are not profitable to them. Already, in the city that Golath has given his own name, they have winnowed out the folk, slaying all who do not bend their necks to the yoke. Some, even of those docile folk, have fled to us for shelter, and we have given them a place, however short-lived, in which to hide. But we know that our own time in our land is short. So we are ready to put our hands and our hearts into the task you choose for us. We know that our own Lords were trustworthy past all reckoning."

Johab smiled at the old man. "Clan-Father, I am joyful to hear your words, but I cannot let my people leap, unwarned, into the dark. There is terrible danger, past that of simple battle and death, in the task that lies before you."

The Elder laid his hands upon his knees and looked straight into the young Lord's eyes. "Be not misled. We are, indeed, fearful. All the years of the lordship of Golath we have lived in terror, even amid our freedom.

"In the sixth season after the overthrow of your kind, the usurpers sent tax-gatherers into the plains. We could not convince them that there were no riches here, no stores of food past that which would hold our village from starvation in the cold season. They could not comprehend why your people had held regard for us, if they could not gain riches thereby.

"In Relah, to the east, a tax-gatherer seized the Eldest and held him under torture, seeking in this way to force goods from his people. As a matter of course, his folk in turn seized the agent and his attendants and put them to death, after due ceremony and in the way of the old law.

"Then the forces of Golath came against them, riding on grinding monsters of metal, bringing terrible weapons that none had seen before. The Old Ones of Relah sent to us, with their last strength and purpose, the manner of their deaths.

"From those weapons came screaming missiles that burst in midair, shattering the village like a dropped egg, burning all that would burn, slaying Elder and weanling without discrimination. Where Relah stood there is a glazen spot in the plain, without life. The waters of the wells are poisoned, and the land for a great space about is tainted with sickness. The small beasts that seek to forage there grow thin and weak, and their fur falls from their backs. None walks where Relah stood, but we do not forget her fate.

"No, Lord, we are not fearless. Yet we are determined to destroy the cause of our fear, if it may be done."

Johab took the hand of the Eldest from his knee and held it between his own. "There is no courage save that of men who are afraid and conquer their fear," he said. "I am honored to be among your people, Clan-Father. There are few of such fortitude among the forces of Golath, you may be sure. The weak and the fearful ride at his tail, and the greedy forage before him. There may yet be hope for the people of the plain.

"But your words of the strange weapon bring sickness to my heart. Know that my folk, the Old Lords, were not always so wise and knowing as they were in our years. Before my earliest grandfathers drew breath, they were seeking for ways to work their will upon all things. They were led astray, so our history tells us, into poisonous error, seeking to manipulate the very stuff of matter. The weapons they made in that time are intolerably destructive. Those who worked with the weapons died, even as would any upon whom they might have used them.

"Still, they were wiser than Golath. They knew the things were unusable by men who walked in the ways of the gods, so they hid them away and made laws proscribing their use. They turned to the limitless power of the sun and the stars for their purposes. They set in the sky the triple moons, that they might have power by night as by day. They turned their thoughts to the well-being of those under their rule, and they forsook war, uniting all the continent in their confederation.

"They made no more poisonous weapons, but they made others, usable by men of good will against those who war upon them . . ."

The Old One's eyes lit with a fierce gleam. "There are, then, weapons to be used against the usurpers? Weapons that might even be more powerful than that which shattered Relah?" he asked eagerly.

"There are, in the south, weapons that the usurpers would tremble to hear of," Johab replied. "They are hidden well, and one other and I hold the keys to their place. But that other is a prisoner in the dungeon of Mirreh."

The Eldest raised his head. "Prisoners may be freed," he said.

8

Out of the Dark Places

THE village was abuzz with activity. Though the sun shone hotly upon the hurrying people, still they moved quickly and with purpose. An aura of fierce joy hung about them. The chosen ones were looked upon with envy by those who must stay behind for the tending of the village and the young and the very old. They walked with conscious pride as they gathered together the weapons and the supplies they had so carefully prepared for the long journey that lay ahead.

They were handsome folk, tall young men and women who had been fully strengthened by the harsh life of the plains. They hoisted their packs upon their shoulders and lifted their weapons effortlessly. Then they stood and waited for the word of Johab.

He and the Eldest lingered within the talking-house, hand set in hand.

"Eldest, I take with me the flower of your village. It is no certain task we attempt, but one full of perils that even I cannot guess. None of us may ever walk the plains again. I ask this final time if this be the will of the Council of Elders," the lad said earnestly.

"Lord, we have lived long in shadow. Would you now take the light of the new-risen sun from us? We have purpose who had none. We have a task pleasing to the gods, we who only scrabbled to keep life in our useless bodies before now. Take our strongest and our best. If they die in service to the gods, it will be a thing of pride, more than of pain, to those of us who stay behind." The old man bowed his head and kissed the hand that held his own.

Johab curved his arm about the thin shoulders and bowed his own head, in turn. "My people were more than fortunate to gain the allegiance of such a folk as yours," he said. Then he turned and left the hut.

Those outside stood patiently in the sun-shimmer, scorning the invitation of leatherwood-shadow that circled each of the houses in the enclave. Their dark heads were high, and their two-score eyes went at once to Johab when he stepped before them. No hand rose in the air, no sound left their lips. They had been schooled in disciplines that made such easy salutes seem childish. They honored Johab in the pride of their stance and in the brightness of their coppery eyes.

In turn, Johab made no sign, spoke no word, but stood gazing upon them, one by one, until he felt that he knew each by face, if not yet by name. Interrupting the silent double-scrutiny, an old woman came from beneath a leatherwood tree into the sunlight. Upon her back she carried a bag, which she laid upon the ground before Johab

"Lord," she said, busily untying the strings, "I have made for you and for our own folk a gift, which I have only just completed. Take these and know more comfort under the sun."

She drew from her bag a pile of hats, woven from the underbark of the leatherwood. Broadbrimmed and deep-crowned, they would shelter their wearers from the fiercest bite of the orange sun. There were precisely twenty-one, and that which she gave to Johab fitted him as though he had been measured for it.

"Clan-Sister, we give you our thanks," he said, taking her

hand. "You have given us that which will speed our journey."

She smiled without a word, then turned and disappeared again beneath the trees. Then there was no person of the village left upon the open space except for those who were to go with Johab.

He lifted his hand, only a slight movement, and took his pack upon his back. The twenty moved as one, and the band walked away into the burning plain. No hand rose to wave them on, no eye watched their departure. The village lay in accustomed quiet, and its folk went about their tasks as if no uncommon thing had taken place.

Overhead, the abreet circled, circled, keeping its bright and mechanical eyes alert for any motion, any speck upon the broad expanse below. Johab would ride with it, now and again, but he preferred to remain anchored firmly in his own flesh, sharing the punishing pace, the terrible heat that his companions bore without complaint or wish for rest.

The first night found them camped in and about one of the rounded copses, whose native plants supplied many of their wants, leaving their emergency stores untouched. Johab sat beneath a leatherwood, his abreet perched above in its crown, to rest himself and repair his boots, which the steady walking was wearing thin. The men and women were busy about their small fires, simmering stews of merryberry and nutroot. All was peaceful.

He stretched his legs and settled his back comfortably against the bole. Then he sent out his seeing self toward the south, feeling along the ways as he went, searching for any taint of danger. And danger there was, many times, as his spirit passed over the plain. As the mountains loomed ahead, he felt the peril increase. Then his mind-touch found Ellora, whom he had not sought these many days, and her welcoming surge of feeling was enough of joy to erase any threat.

Again he was within the dungeon, and now there was no

light at all. Only by the feel and the rattle of chains did he know that Ellora still hung against the wall, her skin caked with filth, her bones crying out in pain, but her self still sharp and bright as jewel light.

"My friend!" he cried to her, in the silent way of their people, "how is it with you?"

"Johab, all is well, now that you have come. These animals think to torture me with darkness, which is a comfort to me. Still, bodies are mortal, and mine is coming near to collapse, I begin to feel. My spirit has begun to beat against the walls of flesh, seeking a way to go free. Twice more have I thought myself into familiar places, only to be seized at once. There is no place to go save into death, and I fear that you find me for the last time."

"No! We are on our way, and nine days will see us here. Can you not wait for us?" Johab asked, his heart weeping.

"Nine days will be, I think, four days too long," she said. "Will can hold my greater to my lesser part for no longer than five more days. Well do I know my capacities, and this is a true estimate."

"Then we will bring you forth now," said her companion.

"But there is no place that I have not tried!" she said, and impatience tinged her thought. "Unless I can see, hear, smell, feel the things of the place, I cannot make it real. How can I go forth?"

"My self lies within a grove, many leagues distant from the mountains. About it are my folk, who are worth many times their number of Mirreh's scourers. My senses can see, hear, feel, smell all the things that are there directly and not through the faulty lens of memory. Send out your thought with me. Know the place where I am. Come!"

Without waiting for reply, he seized her thought, as she had before seized his, and went out in a great rush, over the mountains, down the slopes, across the plain to the copse where his body lay. Willingly, she went. Her joy was great when she saw through his knowledge the far sweep of the plain, the tremendous and unbounded sky where the triple moons spun in mad splendor.

When they alighted and she sat within his own being, she spoke to him again. "My dear friend and kinsman, this is an untried thing we do. My self is weak and ill. You must have the key words, or you would not be here upon the plain with these companions. Let me give to you my part of the key, that it may not be lost. It is, 'There is a stone within, shaped like an arrow. It fits into a slot and turns.' "

"This will give the weapons into our hands," said Johab, "for my part says, 'The Chasm of Genlith; to the right.' "

Then they sank together into a strange state, concentrating upon the things about them. Johab fed into her flagging self all the vitality he had regained since finding his freedom. There was the beginning of a glimmer beside him upon the moss. A shape was forming, slowly, hesitantly, pulsing as though the fires of life within it were flickering. Johab gave of himself until he felt to be a husk, and still the shape struggled to find reality. Then someone came quietly through the shadows and stood beside him. A soft voice said, "Lord, you need the aid of my strength. Take it for your task." A hand took his.

A flood of energy tensed him. He looked up into the dim face above and said, "Clan-Sister, take from my arm the bracelet, drawing your finger through the grooves first round to the right, then left, then across. When it is in your hand, hold it to focus upon me the light of the triple moons."

The shadowy head nodded, and he felt her fingers at his arm. Then the bracelet was gone, and he felt on his face the patterns of light that filled him with strange potencies. The shape beside him grew in substance, gaining weight so that the moss was dented where it lay. It became tangible, warm, alive, but even so it was possible to feel from its emanations that it was terribly fevered and ill.

The girl who held the bracelet exclaimed, "She must be aided!" Her voice rose in a call that was answered by the appearance of two of her sisters.

"May we give help, Ruthan?" one of them asked.

The tall girl brushed a wisp of coppery hair from her cheek and bent over Ellora. "Quickly, Selot, build up the fire and dig for water roots. There is one here whom the Lord has brought forth from the air, and she is ailing."

Johab looked down at the girl who lay beside him. Thin, filthy, ragged as she was, she had the tough beauty of his own people. The mop of curling brown hair matched his own, and when, for a fleeting moment, her eyes opened, he saw the silvery steel of her glance before she slipped into unconsciousness. He thought her a few years older than he, and the thought comforted him. With two of the Old Lords left in the lands, much could be done.

Johab smiled and relaxed against the earth and his tree bole. His work was finished, for now. He chuckled inwardly, thinking of Mirreh's face when he found his dungeon empty once more and no trace of his captive in all the lands he held.

Now Ellora was in competent hands. He had no doubt that Ruthan and her sisters would make her comfortable and well, given time. He sighed deeply and sank into sleep, leaving his people to their tasks.

The three women quietly cleaned the unconscious Ellora, treated her wounds, then waited. Though they marveled at the way in which she had been brought among them, they were unsurprised. The Old Lords were expected to perform miracles.

9

Empty Dungeons

Golath, Benevolent and Omnipotent Lord of the City and the Plain, was quite simply terrified. For seven years he had held the scion of Enthala, the last survivor of all the families of the Old Lords in the north of Rehannoth. In that time neither persuasion nor coercion had forced anything of value from the recalcitrant youngster. Being a more kindly man than his career might have indicated, he had resisted the insistence of his co-conspirator in the south that he execute the lad and thus make sure that he was no threat to the new coalition of powers.

Marveling that one so young could show such fortitude, he had used every bit of guile at his command when the furious and grief-stricken nine-year-old had been brought to the city. When that was not efficacious, he had applied many kinds of pressures, using the techniques devised by the clever men who had flocked about him at once, when his power was secured. After seven years of combined temptation, torture and solitary confinement, the youth had still been as adamant as he had been that first day.

And now the troublesome young man was gone from his cell. No trace of him remained. No scratch marked the metal walls. The door slot was totally secure, its seals intact. The food slot was too small for a cat to enter. After all the years of denying that his people had or used exotic devices, the boy had, at once, proven that his captors were correct in their beliefs and that he was a master of whatever devices there were.

Which was bad enough, in all truth. However, worse than all was the prospect of informing Mirreh—Mirreh of the cold eyes and the steel-trap mouth—that the captive that he had refused to kill was free upon the plain, conjuring up hideous plots and conspiracies against the new Lords of Rehannoth.

Golath sighed and scrubbed a knuckle against his nose, an invariable habit in time of stress. Lijeh, his current favorite, offered him wine, fruit, caresses, all of which he refused gruffly.

In three days, the weekly conference with Mirreh was due to take place. The glass and metal communicators that had been his pride and boast were now hateful to him. If their inventor had still been alive, he would have had him skinned. How could he possibly inform his valued friend and hated rival that he had failed in such an important responsibility? And Mirreh would be furious, he well knew. That cutting tongue would once more be aimed at Golath's sensitive ego, wounding him to the core.

Once more, he took himself ponderously to the deeps where the metal cells had been constructed to his own specifications. They were still impregnable, invulnerable, impossible to escape from, by any sane standard. The door slot was set in the ceiling, and the tenant of the cell was lowered into his prison. The food slot was too small for even a large portion of food to enter. The walls were seamless metal, hardened to admirable strength. None had ever escaped from them, and many had lived and died in their horrible isolation.

Johab! Hated name of a hated youth! How he wished that he had poisoned him while he had the opportunity!

As he gazed down at his handiwork from the special cat-walk that he had had constructed for his inspections, a member of his own Guard approached cautiously and saluted him with a deep bow.

"Rise," said Golath in the languid voice he affected as befitting a nobleman. "You have a message for me?"

"Lord," quavered the sweating soldier, "there is news from the plain."

Golath looked at the man with sharp attention now, noting his obvious fear and distress. "What news? Quickly, man!"

"A terrible cloud was seen far to the east, some days ago, by those who watch the plain at the edge of the farmlands. They sent men out to find its cause, for the day was clear and the cloud seemed to be dust rising from the ground.

"There is a new valley blown into the face of the plain. Those who were sent to find—to find *him*—are gone from the land, and only fragments show that they were ever there at all. Worse than all, the weapon that was sent with them is gone, also. It is thought by your craftsmen that the weapon was triggered in some way to destroy itself. Possibly." The man fell silent, and sweat rolled down his face.

Golath turned and motioned to the guard beside him. A slit opened and the unfortunate soldier was hurled into one of the cells below.

If he had been unhappy before, now he was in torment. To lose the weapon of the Old Lords, the only one they had found in operating condition in any of the holds, the key to control of the free folk of the plain, was a sin that Mirreh would not forgive, he felt certain.

Could it be concealed? He doubted that it could, for he felt sure that Mirreh had placed spies in the City of Golath, just as Golath had placed spies in Olanthe. Trust was a thing for fools and children. Among men of the world, men of power, it could not exist.

Gnawing a wisp of his carefully-groomed blond beard, he turned from his vantage point and hurried through his ornate marble corridors toward the center of the stronghold. Behind him, guards clacked rapidly, trying to keep up with the billowing tail of his robe. At the door of his secret study, he bellowed back to the quivering men, "Call the Elder of the city. Call the General of the Guard. Call the Chief Technician. At once. Here." He swirled from sight, and the door closed sharply behind him.

He had regained some of his composure by the time the Elder rang the chime beside his door. "Enter," he said in the deep voice he had practiced in order to emulate the Old Lord whom he had betrayed.

"L . . . lord," stammered the Elder, and his ruler knew that the title still stuck in his throat, even after so many years. Perhaps it had been an error on his part—and Mirreh's, also—to assume that title. Every time one of his subjects used it, he could feel them remembering their lives under his predecessors. Master of Life and Death might well have been better and more accurate. But it was too late to remedy.

"Has there been rumor in the city today? Any kind or sort of tale told by idlers who should be at the treadmills or carrying stone for my fortifications?" He watched the old man closely as he searched for an answer.

The Elder bowed again, his white straggles of hair almost brushing the floor. "Lord, there is always talk. Some have even said . . . ridiculous tale, and I said so immediately . . . that there had been an escape from the metal cells. Not to mention the fact that some days ago a terrible cloud appeared in a clear sky, far, far to the East. Such a thing always brings out superstitious nonsense. But there is nothing to give you concern."

"Take ten of my guard with you. Point out to them everyone who has mentioned this vicious nonsense. Let it be known that any who give lip to such will be my guest in the metal cells. Hear me well, old man. I will not tolerate such behavior."

The Eldest bowed yet again, but his shrewd old brain was putting things together. "So, there *has* been an escape!" he said to himself as he moved nervously ahead of the ten guards. "We have known that he held the Lord Johab. Only he might have found a way to make such an escape."

He shivered, though the day was already hot. The thought of the manner in which he and most of his folk had betrayed the teaching of the Old Lords often gave him nightmares. Now, added to that, was the thought that he was about to betray into the metal cells some dozen or so of his own citizens. Well did he know that they would never be heard from again. Even rumor did not penetrate so far as the interior of the complex that held those cells. Fear was the only fact left in his world.

Behind him, in the complex dome of Golath's palace, the Chief Guard was already being hustled toward imprisonment in those selfsame cells, and the Chief Technician was putting on a bold face as he entered Golath's lair.

As he bent his back, Golath spoke. "You have heard what has occurred. You will not convey it to anyone, or allow your underlings to do so. Your family is already in my hands. They will go to the torturers if any word of the escape goes outside the walls of my city. Do you understand?"

The man blanched. His comfortable life, the luxuries he had prided himself upon giving his wife and sons, shivered away into irrelevance. He knew his Lord.

"Your will is my law," he gasped.

"Then go. And remember." Golath watched him go, a grin of cruel satisfaction hidden behind his beard. Then he thought of Mirreh, and he shuddered, himself. He realized, not for the first time, that there was not room enough for two New Lords on the lonely continent of Rehannoth.

Mirreh approached the dungeons with more than usual anticipation. His captive had tried twice more to escape and had been brought back immediately each time. Surely by now she would be amenable to suggestion. He had ordered that she be

neither fed nor given opportunity to clean herself in the days
since her last escape, and he felt that by now her physical condition would force her to cooperate or to die.

Harl, the jailor, kindled the torch at the watchfire in the
guard room.

Mirreh's sallow face jerked into a smirk as he said, "Take
the keys, Harl. It is likely that we shall bring her out with us,
by now. She cannot possibly have much life left in her. This
time I will win. My mother insisted that I would fail at this,
arguing that my methods were entirely wrong. It will be a fine
thing to send for her from her exile and tell her that I won!
I won!"

The scarred jailor said nothing but turned on his heel and
led the way into the tunnels. The sound of water dripping and
of rats scrabbling away from the light masked any sound the
prisoner might have made. No moan or gasp or sigh could be
heard in the place.

They rounded the last bend. Harl held the torch high, and
its light glinted on the damp and rusty shackles that hung,
empty, from the wall.

"Again! She cannot have gone again! She was too weak
and worn, after the last time and the beatings, to have energy
to escape! She has had help! Harl!"

The jailor turned his hideous face and gazed upon his master. The light flowed down his huge arm, making the muscles
seem to crawl with power. The enigmatic look in his eyes,
coupled with the effect of the drawn-down eyelid that half
covered his right eye, quenched the accusation in the thin
man's throat.

"We must make inquiry among those in the mountains. She
will be in one of those spots she knew well, as always. Come.
We will go up and begin our search again."

Harl said nothing, but his lip drew down to match his eyelid, and Mirreh knew in his innermost heart that he feared
this one man more than any he knew. So he hurried again

into the light and climbed the stair to his Center of Communications, where he found a worried technician waiting for him.

"Lord, there is word from the spy in Golath's City. The young Johab has escaped from the metal cells. Though Golath himself should have sent the word, he is waiting, our spy said, for the regular day of communication.

"Our man says that there is rumor of even worse loss, but he has been unable to learn of its nature. Shall we call upon Golath beforetime?"

Mirreh opened his mouth to agree. Then he thought of his own discovery of the morning and closed it again. "Not at this time. There are reasons of . . . strategy. . . that make it inadvisable to reveal that we know of this. Attend closely to the equipment, Erthol. If our spy reports again, let me know immediately. And call me at the regular time for my conference with Golath. We will pretend that we know nothing. And see if he tells us the truth, eh?" He smirked at the young man, who grinned nervously back at his master.

Mirreh quivered internally with frustration. He had waited for long to find an excuse for quarrelling with Golath. He felt that his own forces were superior to any that his fellow-conspirator could muster, and he knew that he was the logical ruler of the entire domain of the Old Lords. If only Golath's losses had come at another time, when they could not be countered with his own misfortune!

They had been in agreement on one point, he and Golath. Ellora, being a few years older than Johab, was the more valuable captive. By the nature of things, she would have been trained longer and would have had access to more advanced secrets than her young kinsman. And, being a woman, she should have been easier to coerce. She was to live. But the boy, he had always felt, ought to be killed. And here was proof.

The seven years since their successful rebellion had proved them both wrong about Ellora now, he had admitted privately to himself. Neither of the surviving Lords had given one moment's consideration to either bribe or threat. Nothing that had been done to them had made them waver. It seemed that they were not really attached to their bodies by any very firm ties, for whatever it was that made them individuals had appeared to depart temporarily when their flesh was overly stressed.

And now Ellora was gone again. This time, Mirreh had a doleful premonition, was different from the others. Every time she had been caught and returned, it had been before her captors had known that she was gone. Now he felt a terrible certainty that she was indeed gone from his sphere of power.

He paced his study, biting his lower lip. How his mother would mock him! She was proven, once again, to be correct in her beliefs and advice, and the fact galled him past endurance. It was shameful enough that she had been the motive force behind the entire rebellion. He hid from himself, most of the time, the fact that he would never have had either the courage or the brilliance to foment a secret revolution among those who were envious of the Old Lords without her constant encouragement and counsel.

And now he must face Golath and admit that he, too, had lost a key to the secret power of the Old Lords. It would leave him with no advantage, no excuse for pushing the other into open war. They must still talk in hateful harness, the two of them distrusting and disliking one another past the point of endurance.

A messenger touched the crystal bell beside the door-curtain. "It is time for the communication with Golath, Lord."

Mirreh sighed. Now he must face Golath and match him lie for lie.

10

Into Peril

ELLORA woke slowly, her mind seeming to rise through many-layered waters, surfacing a sense at a time into life again. Her body knew comfort. Pain was still with her, as natural to her by now as breathing. But transcending that there was ease of limb and bone. A warm breeze touched her face, and her cheek lay upon softness.

"I am among the happy mad," she said, and her own voice woke her fully. Her eyes opened upon treetops waving in air, blue-pale sky, shafts of orange sunlight. An abreet perched high, its rounded shape moving her to smile at old memories. There was someone near, and she turned her head to see.

"Do not move, Lord," said a soft voice. "You must rest long and eat well. Your body must heal. From whatever place our Lord brought you, you have come in sickness and injury.

"I am Ruthan of the plainsfolk. My kin and I fare forth with the Lord Johab against the usurpers. We know you to be of the folk of our Lord, and we serve you, also." Ruthan laid her hand upon Ellora's forehead, then nodded with satisfaction.

"Your fever is less. Could you eat now?"

Ellora thought for a moment. "It has been long since I tasted food fit for human folk. The slops Mirreh serves would sicken a scavenger. If the smell the winds bring to me is that of food, then I will willingly eat."

While she ate, half sitting propped against packs, Johab woke and rose from his place. "My friend," he said, kneeling beside her, "how do you fare this fine and free morning?"

Their eyes met and glowed with joy, as she answered, "Truly, Johab, I am well, indeed, in the hands of your ladies. They have cleansed my skin and tended my wounds and filled my inward parts with broth and bread. What other comforts can any reasonable being wish for?"

"Only for the freedom of our lands and our people," he answered, and she nodded. Then he turned to Ruthan and said, "Clan-Sister, call our people to us, that we may consult and find what is best to do. Bring also those who speak inwardly with the Elders, for they must keep them informed, that they may not worry unduly."

By the time he had finished his frugal meal, the warrior-folk were gathered within the shadow of the little wood, waiting for his words. When he stood, they fell silent. He looked upon them with affection.

"My kinsmen, we have gone forth to bring dismay upon the tyrants who have seized our land. Upon all this planet, there is no land but this continent, large as it is, to give us a home, so we must make this place fit for living. We came, firstly, as the Elders told you, to bring from the southern keeps one who could aid us in finding weapons fit to shake the hold of the usurpers from our throats. Now this has been done in a way never used before, even by my kind. We did not need to show ourselves to our enemies in any way. Thus, we are much farther upon our road than we had cause to think we might be when we set out.

"Yet there will be much outcry, there in the south, when the Lord Ellora is found to be missing. Some of the devices of our fathers are in the hands of Mirreh and his like, we surmise, and these things can scan afar, seeing any movement.

We must remain hidden from the air for a span of several days . . . perhaps one hand of days will be enough.

"For this time we must scatter to other copses and hide within them, resting and storing strength against the future. In this time, the Lord Ellora may heal and regain strength that she may lend her powers to us as we lend ours to her. In this way we will double our chances of success.

"The hands of the gods are aiding us. This I feel to be true. Your own Old Ones have felt the same. There will be freedom again upon the lands of Rehannoth."

The listeners stood quiet. Then one stepped forth and said, "Lord, we follow. If fortune and the gods aid us, we are happy. But if death and defeat stand before us, still, we follow."

Ellora raised herself upon her cushioned pallet and said, "There are in the hands of Mirreh some few of the abreet. When none of the people round about Olanthe bring word of me, the tyrant will look afar, toward the seacoast and the mountains and the plain. He will send the abreet to help him in his search. It would be well, I think, if we find our hiding places now, before the abreet are in the air. What food needs no cooking, we should share out, for smoke will fetch unwelcome company."

Johab nodded agreement. "We must become part of the leatherwood and the dallbush, for a time. Divide yourselves as you please, but take great care if need drives you across the plain to another copse. Night will be our ally in this. Go, my friends, and make ready for a rest."

It seemed to Ellora that the folk melted away into the air, so soon were they gone. The cookfires were quenched, the food eaten or shared out. Soon parties were trudging away into the plain, aiming their steps toward one or another of the copses visible in the distance. Before the sun had touched zenith, the plain lay in an empty shimmer before her eyes. Even Johab's abreet, from the cool heights to which they sent him, could not detect their presence among the thick-branched leatherwoods.

The day wore on, but to Ellora the passage of the time was not tiresome. The play of leaves above her, the movements of the plainsfolk about the copse, the heavy heat reflected beneath the trees from the scorching plain, all were newly discovered and comforting to her bruised spirit. To lie at ease, her flayed wrists and ankles wrapped with balms, in the light of day, with one at her side who was of her own kind, these things were new-minted and more than valuable.

For a long time she slept after midday, but as the sun slanted downward, she roused and sat, staring southward. Johab, who had been dozing nearby, sat also and looked at her sharply.

"Call in the abreet," she said suddenly. "Do you not feel movement in the air? Mirreh's eyes are moving upon the plain, and there must be nothing here to see."

Johab closed his eyes for a moment. The abreet plummeted down through the foliage to light above his head.

"There in the south . . . I felt a tremor, a moving, but I could not surely know its nature," he said.

The girl laughed. "You have not lived as long as I, or so closely with our lord to the south. I feel the worms of his thoughts crawling in the dungheap of his mind. Surely I feel the abreet of my father when they take wing, even when they are directed by and scanned through awkward devices of metal and glass. No mind guides them now, only a generated impulse from the ridiculous mechanisms that Mirreh has had his people make. They see, not with their own seeing thought that rides with the bird, but with pulses of power that make images upon glass. Yet those who do this believe that they have begun to conquer the sciences of the Old Lords with such toys."

Johab frowned. "Those who have no knowledge of the powers within themselves must rely upon such, my father used to say. Yet such things can be deadly, as all our folk learned at great cost. One cannot sense a machine as it works, as you can sense a mind. You must find through physical means where it is, what it does, and when it is working. Then you may send your thought to read it, but much time and energy must be wasted in the effort. Devices can work against us tirelessly, unlike living beings who must rest. Do not weigh them lightly in the balance, for they were the key that unlocked our doors to the tyrants. They and the traitors who had taken service in our houses."

Ellora had tensed, her eyes searching the sky to the south, what part of it could be seen through the concealing branches. "They are coming," she said. "I will send my thought to ride with them . . . surely the coarse powers that command them cannot feel so light a touch?"

"I think not," said Johab, and he moved to sit beside her and take her hand.

Her thought winged outward, Johab's following. Far they went, across the dappled plain, until the felt the purr that was an abreet below them in the air. Then they were seeing through the eye-cells of the device as it quartered the sky, wheeling above each copse, watching closely all the open space below.

There was a tingling thrum of power surging in the device. Ellora's thought touched Johab's. "They do not know that it can draw power from the sun. Even though our people made the knowledge open to any who wished to learn, these dark-minded folk could not trust anything that was not hidden and twisted. This is a thing to hold in thought, for it shows how limited their minds must be."

They swung with the abreet over the plain, dipping and soaring, edging ever nearer to the places where their people lay concealed. Closely and carefully they scanned the copses through the alien abreet eyes, as they passed. No trace of an unwonted presence could they see. The abreet moved beyond, quartering each area of the land, but Johab and Ellora returned to themselves in the shadows and lay resting, at peace.

For three days the skies were specked, near or far, with the abreet, but no untoward movement or trace upon the earth betrayed the presence of the plainsfolk. At last the things were gone into the south, called by their new lord to search other ways. Then the people among the copses again prepared to move.

Even then they made no rash start in dawnlight. With falling darkness they left their sheltering groves and went out into the plains, taking care to smooth away their footprints from the dusty places, sweeping them clear with branches brought for the purpose. With Johab and Ellora seeking ahead with their seeing thoughts, they moved speedily toward the distant mountains. When the sun rose again upon the horizon, filling the east with its swollen red bulk, they were at rest in a large grove that had stretched across their way.

But there was unease among them. Some dim dread lay on their hearts, nudging at their senses. The two Lords sat together, wordless. Ellora felt the malaise about them as almost a tangible thing.

"I know little of the lands beyond our mountains, Johab," she said at last. "What perils do they hold for the unwary? My father never spoke to me of any such dread as this, though he had traveled in all parts of Rehannoth and knew all the lands.

"In the northern plains I can name every danger that might arise. I was still very young when the usurpers struck, and I had not yet been sent into the southern places. There is something in the lands before us that fills me with dread, but I cannot name it or tell how to pass it in safety."

The terrible sun was again upon the horizon, and they made ready to sleep. None of them, Lords or plainsfolk, slept deeply or easily; something waited, out on the plain beyond the grove, and they dreamed ill of what it might be. When the edge of darkness again touched the sky, they rose gladly and made their cold meal.

As they went from the shelter of the grove, chill drops began to patter into the dust. That edge of darkness had concealed a wrack of cloud that moved swiftly from the western ocean, carrying with it one of the infrequent but violent storms that raked the plains with wind and rain and lightning in the hot months. Only seconds behind the first spatter of rain came a sough of wind that bowed the tall grove deeply and caused the travelers to cling desperately to their packs, which caught gusts and tried to overbalance them. Lightning hissed and crackled before them, and they knew that at least one leatherwood, at least one copse might well perish in the fires from the sky.

Ellora stood facing the rising storm, her hair lashing behind her. By the filtered light that glanced through the cloud from the moons, Johab could see she was smiling.

"Never again did I think to stand amid the tumult of the sheeash in the clean wind and the free rain. Let us go forward. No abreet can fly, no searcher will venture out into such a storm."

So they went, heads bent, seeking a sure footing as the dust turned rapidly to mud. The storm settled, after a time, into a steady, pounding rain. The wind died to a breeze, whipping water into their ears and down their necks. Speed was impossible, but their steady pace did not falter. They had covered several leagues when Ruthan stopped, causing her husband, just behind her, to stumble into her.

Her head was up, her eyes seeking desperately into the darkness ahead.

"Lords," she said, above the drumming of the rain, "we must stop. There is something there, just before us, that fills my heart with terror. It is death, and the dead cannot accomplish our task." She stood trembling in the darkness, her husband's arm about her as Johab and Ellora came near.

"We must have light," said Johab. "It would be ill to remain beside such danger in the darkness. It would be foolish to go blindly forward after such warning."

Ellora was fumbling in her pack. "Here is my lightglass that you lent me, Clan-Sister. We will see what bars our way."

The spark-wheel of the glass was damp, and it took many flicks to kindle it to flame. In the blackness that now wrapped the plain, the tiny spark made no impression upon the wet void that stretched before them. Then the two Lords loosed from their arms their bracelets. Joining hands, they had Ruthan hold up the lightglass so that its spark shone out through the aligned crystals.

A blaze of light answered their efforts. The pudding-like mud of the plain glistened and winked as the raindrops lit; the rain itself shone as a bright curtain of many strands. And through that curtain gazed . . . something. In a heaving wallow forty strides away in the sea of mud terrible shapes writhed and lumped themselves upward, as though disturbed by the light. Then a wormlike shape sorted itself from the mass and began to loop itself across the mud, seeming to seek the light.

As if inspired by its example, the other creatures ceased their gamboling and followed, eyes winking in the light, sides shining obscenely, heads weaving with their efforts. The folk stood, rooted with horror, as the creatures moved. Then Ellora and Johab jerked their hands apart. The light dimmed to one spark, and the sounds of squishing and shlooping died away.

"We must go back to the last copse," whispered Johab. "Here where the mud is thick those things can come to us. Perhaps the clutter in the grove may stay them, if they should follow us."

"But what are they, Lord?" gasped Ruthan, her shaking stilled by shock.

"My father told me of them, or of something so like them I

cannot make out the difference. They are called mud-suckers, and they can suck the flesh from a man's bones in a few heartbeats. They lie dormant in the earth of the plain until the winter rains or a sudden sheeash revives them. They swim through the wet soil as do the water creatures through the sea. Let us put leagues between ourselves and those creatures!"

More swiftly than they had come, they returned through the wet and the mud to the last copse they had passed and went gratefully to earth beneath the shelter of its trees. In short moments, they had taken from their packs the parts of shelters and were protected from the rain. Cold rations were taken; then they fell into sleep, leaving the two Lords to watch with their inner vision.

The night wore along slowly for them. Ellora huddled against Johab's back, straining to feel through the darkness for motion or life. But the plain was a moil of motion as waters fell and wind blew, and any moving life was lost within it.

When light crept over the horizon, the two were cold and stiff, weary to the bone. They stirred themselves, stood, and went to the edge of the grove to look southward. They needed to look no farther than a bowshot to find the enemy they sought. A curve of wallowing shapes circumscribed their sanctuary. A glitter of eyes caught the light of the sky.

"Johab!" said Ellora, sharply. "If any abreet are aloft in these skies today they will see something amiss. If the rain continues to fall from that watery sky, these things will remain with us. From the air, it will be plain that the mudsuckers have surrounded potential prey. We must find a way to return them, if only for a time, to their dormant state."

"Aye," grunted Johab. "The others are waking. Let us think together. I believe I know a way, but it may be unacceptable to my people."

Now the plainsfolk were stirring in the copse, and the two Lords called them together beneath the largest of the leatherwoods that crowned the rounded oasis. Johab stood forward and raised his hand. They quieted to listen.

"We are caught in a ring of the mud-beasts," he said. "In the night, they came and surrounded us, though they could not come through the drier and matted soil beneath the trees. If the tyrant to the south again turns his abreet to the plains, they will know that the track that encircles this wood must contain an enemy. It will say to them very clearly that someone walks upon the lands of their domain. We are not yet armed to battle the usurpers. They will come upon us and overwhelm us. We will find death, which will not serve our people, or slavery, which will not serve our souls."

Ruthan's husband, Jearth, raised his head. "Is there nothing to do, Lord, but to die or to be enslaved?"

"I can find only one thing to do that may save our mission. It is a terrible act, one against all our hearts' instincts, against the teachings of our youth, against the very nature of the life the gods have given us. It is a thing that I do not ask you to help me do. If you decide against it, I will wait with you for the turn of our fate, and I will say nothing to chide you.

"We must fire the grove." Johab watched as the folk swayed, and a great gasp went up from them. They looked at one another, then into the sheltering branches above them.

Ruthan turned to the two Lords. "Will this surely allow us to go upon our way?"

Ellora shook her head. "No thing is sure, this side the veil of death," she said. "Yet with our crystals and our training, we can perhaps heat a segment of the circle of suckers to the point at which they will dry and go into their sleep. Then we may flee. It may be that we can outrun them until the rain ends. It may be that they will catch up with us upon the plain. Or the sun may break through the cloud. It is in the hands of the gods."

The folk gathered in little groups, talking, some of them weeping. Ellora touched Johab's elbow. "My brother, I know the copses are life to the plainsfolk, but why are they so disturbed at the thought of destroying just one, when there are so many?"

Johab smiled at her, but his face was grim with pain, the smile a travesty. "Each grove is a living thing, as you or I," he said. "They are, indeed, life to the plains people, yet they are more. They are the temples wherein we worship the gods. They are, in a strange way, the places where the gods reach forth and touch us with the joy of their ways. We love them, each one alone and all together."

They stood in silence, waiting upon the people.

At last, Huthear, of the House of the Elders, came to them and said, "We have spoken together. We have touched the thought of the Old Ones at home. If only our lives were to be lost, we would die here. There are other considerations, however. No grove, no village, no one of our people may look to continued life as long as the usurpers hold Rehannoth in their grasp. We must go forth and accomplish the task you have set us, Lord. Therefore, we have agreed that the grove must be fired."

There were tears in his eyes as he laid his hand upon the shoulder of his leader. Johab touched Huthear's hand with his own. Then he turned and called, "We will make celebration in the names of the gods. We will bless this grove and send it, perhaps, into the world of the gods."

The faces of the people lightened. They began to gather dry tinder from beneath logs and bark, to rake aside mats of wet leaves to find the dryer layers. Soon there was a great pile of debris beneath the central leatherwood, heaped about its trunk.

Johab laid his hand against the trunk and looked up into its crown. "Friend of the people, we have rested in your shelter, given freely as always. We have eaten the berries of your grove, drunk the waters of the roots and tubers. Now we must send you to pain and death, feeling that thus we serve the purposes of the gods in the only we we know. We do this with utmost pain and sorrow. A part of us will go with you into the smoke and the sky. Go to the gods; go in the fires of peace."

Ruthan touched her lightglass to the pile, which burst into crackles, dimmed as it found dampness, then responded to her fanning with a steady purr.

"Now we must hasten," cried Ellora. "All the folk to the edge of the copse! Johab, lend your crystal to mine!"

At the edge of the wide lands they waited. Behind them the leatherwood thundered into flame, a towering column of glory. The lesser trees and the bushes caught, and soon the entire wood was awash with fire. Then Ellora and Johab joined their crystals again, focusing that terrible heat and light upon a narrow section of the circle of waiting terrors.

For a time, the beasts within the spot of concentrated light seemed unaffected. Then their wallowing became erratic, began to slow. Their great eyes dulled, a bit at a time, as each lobe winked into sleep. As the heat behind the travelers grew more and more intense, the path before them became less perilous. The suckers to right and to left continued their heaving, but none strayed into the territory of its neighbor. Not one of them seemed aware that a part of their number was falling into sleep.

As the flames neared their heels, the hair singed upon their necks, the people and the Lords fled into the plains, crossing over the wallowed mud, stepping upon the very backs of the mud-suckers as they lay rigid in dormancy. They did not slow to look back but sped through the wet air and the mud-swirled land as though it were firm and dry.

The leagues lost in the night were made up in short space of time. No track of their own feet or the creatures' crawling was there to follow, for the rain of the night had washed the land clean. They went southward at all speed, and behind them the pillar of light and smoke was soon lost in the murk of the day.

11

The Chasm of Genlith

SWIFTLY as the travelers moved, the day moved more swiftly still. The cloud wrack broke into drifts, then wisps, before the growing power of the sun. Now the plains ran with ocherous light, and the clouds hung stained with orange fires.

The Lords moved in a terrible tension, driving their bodies without mercy as they strained their senses to rake the skies above, seeking any sensing of abreet. But nothing moved above or below the horizon, and their own abreet circled ahead, held low for concealment, scanning the earth for any nest of mud-suckers that might lie on their way.

They all felt exposed, abroad in the light of day beneath the very porch of the enemy's house. The foothills had drawn nearer, shaping their details at the edge of sight. The mountains loomed behind them, more menacing than ever. The air was cooling, even on the plain in the full sun heat, for they were now climbing the imperceptible slopes of the land toward the heights. More than one of the folk shivered as he walked, and even the Lords felt an oppression of the spirit.

Before noon they had covered many leagues and passed many copses. Then Johab called a halt beneath the grateful shade of the last small grove that could be seen upon their way.

"Our abreet sees no other trees upon the plain. Our next

place of rest will be in the foothills, so we must take our rest now, gathering our strength for a great effort. Tonight must see us travel as the sheeash. Tomorrow must see us hidden in the hills. We are nearing the beginning of our task."

He set aside his pack and moved to help in the building of a small blaze for cooking. The folk moved about him, making ready for food and rest.

In a short time the encampment had settled to rest, but the two Lords lay upon their sleeping pads, side by side, hands clasped, eyes closed, communing without uttered words.

"The Chasm of Genlith," mused Ellora. "I have not heard the name since I was a child. Once, on a journey, I remember my father's seneschal asking him if he would turn aside to visit the Chasm of Genlith. He said there was no need, that he would know if anything there needed his attention. Help me, Johab, to retrace that journey, in my memory. Perhaps I shall find what we need to know."

Then they sank into stillness. Their spirits moved in memory, and bells tinkled about them as pack beasts plodded behind their leaders; voices long lost from human ears cried out gaily; the brightly painted cart upon which rode the daughter of Lord Jornaval swayed delightfully as it rolled along the rutted track. Ahead strode the Lord himself, walking with easy strides, head bent to catch the words of the seneschal, who walked beside him, his shorter legs laboring.

"That is . . . was . . . Suneath, the seneschal," whispered that which was Ellora. "He is asking the question now. Look about, as my head turns, and find some landmark that we may fix upon."

Eagerly, they followed the gaze of the child upon the cart, searching the way for a reference point. To the right, the breast of a mountain sloped upward, clad in ragged tufts of purple blossom and scraggy stands of evergreen. To the left, a sharp bend in the track ahead showed a steep drop to an unseen but noisy stream below in the deeps. The procession moved without haste, peacefully enjoying the warm summer day, the spicy scent of the conifers in full sunlight, the dreamy well-being that seemed to encompass the world.

As they began to round the bend, a notch opened up in the circling height, and one lone peak stood framed in its V. At the straightening of the way, a track, little-used and over-grown, turned, switching down the abrupt slope in drunken loops.

The child bounced excitedly on the seat of the cart as the great declivity came into view. Leaning over the side, she peered down, scooting farther and farther over the side of the cart. Then a firm hand seized the tail of her gown and hauled her back again.

"Much good you'll be to your poor father at the bottom of the deepest chasm in the southern lands," said a gruff voice, as she was set upright and shaken firmly into neatness by the stern old woman who sat beside her. "Now sit still and let me drive, or this idiot beast will have us both down there."

With a sigh of regret, Ellora released the memory. She and Johab opened their eyes.

"That was Hamath, my friend and nurse," she said, and her voice was sad. "They killed her, but only after much diffi-culty. She fought as a she-beast for her cub. We were alone, back-to-back, at the last, and I felt her die. The next moment I was struck from behind and woke to find myself a prisoner in my father's house, in the hands of Mirreh."

"But we have found our guiding peak," said Johab. "That scarred pinnacle, narrow as it is, will be easy to recognize, even from a different angle of vision. The track that led downslope must be the way to the chasm itself. We have done well, this day. Now we must sleep." He turned on his side and touched her cheek gently. "Let none but lovely dreams visit you, Ellora."

She smiled and closed her eyes. "Time enough for lovely

dreams when our task is done," she said. "Let us dream of war, Johab, and of the deaths of tyrants."

They slept deeply until the setting of the sun was signaled by the abreet, which perched above them in the tallest leatherwood. His *"Breeerp!"* brought the Lords to instant wakefulness.

No time was lost in making ready for the long trek, and the last of the light saw the party setting out toward the hills that loomed as a dark mass on the horizon.

The memory of that night remained as a blur in the minds of those who sped through it for all the rest of their lives. The protest of muscles, the wearying of limbs, the growling of hungry bellies were ignored. At the limit of endurance, they harried themselves across that last wide stretch of plain, resting only when some of their number began to fall between step and step. Yet such were the plainsfolk that no word of complaint passed their lips, even when they fell. And the Lords matched step for step, league for league, though both had been so recently imprisoned. The training of their youth, which had stood by them in their long years of imprisonment, held them to their task.

When the sun again cast its forerunners of flame into the eastern sky, the folk were safely hidden in the shelter of the hills, deep in a tree-bordered ravine where even a cookfire could not be seen from land or air. Long they slept, and so deeply that even the Lords left no sense awake to feel across the hills for the approach of an enemy. For all knew themselves to be at the edge of exhaustion. Rest was more important, for the time, than caution.

Now came a time of wariness increased to the utmost. The Lords honed their senses against the mountain wind. The abreet circled carefully, low amid the trees of the foothills, conning their path among the ravines and ridges that flowed down the hills from the heights above.

The chill of the higher lands troubled them, after the heat of the plain, and they welcomed the sun with joy each morning. Feeling themselves hidden in the dense forest, they traveled by day again, though the Lords felt that others moved about the hills by ones and twos, tending beasts and gathering fuel. They took care not to come near anyone who might make his own death by seeing their passage.

The days passed, and they moved up and up, climbing through the fresh-scented trees into the edges of the mountains. When their view was at last unobstructed by the forest, they could see, away to the right, a lone sharp peak, narrow as a spindle, that would guide them to the Chasm of Genlith.

Now they came upon roads that wound among the heights. These they avoided, picking their way along precipitous slopes and among uncertain scree, in order that they might not be seen by any of their enemies' people. So when they came at last to the road of Ellora's memory, they were a scratched and bruised band, worn to the bone with effort.

But there the road was, curling away before them to follow the curve of the unseen chasm below. They followed it around the curve and saw with joy the mouth of the steep track that led into the depths.

The orange sun was near setting behind them as they approached the track. Their shadows strode before them, giant-wise, angling strangely upon the rocky slope that bordered their way. The warm light turned the pinnacle to fairy-gold, and the purple shadows were wells of chill as they went into the turning, as into a tunnel, leaving the light behind. The steep descent began.

Ellora and Johab led the way. The abreet spiraled downward ahead of them, seeking for any of the enemy's people who might be there. But there was no life there except for the small beasts that lived in the crannies of the rock walls, and the creatures of the water in the cold and rushing stream that had cut the chasm in the process of its long running.

At the end of the pathway there was an apron of level rock, curved neatly as a porch, set into the cliffside. At one edge of this level spot was a notch, visible to anyone standing at the proper spot. This was soon discovered by Ruthan, who was looking about for a way to get down to the water below.

"Lords!" she called. "I have found a path."

The two hurried to her side and peered down the breakneck trace that spanned the drop to the river. Johab looked at Ellora.

"The Chasm of Genlith, to the right," he said.

They turned to the people. "We must go into the depths," said Ellora. "If we succeed in what we must do, then we will need all your aid, for many things must be brought up from below. Await us here and rest. If we perish, go back to your folk with our love and blessing."

The two turned to the path, which was no more than shallow footholds upon protruding stones and toeholds in crevices and fingerholds in narrow cracks. Still, they inched their way downward, never looking into the depths below them. At last they knew by the sound of the water that they neared the bottom.

Johab, who led, looked down and saw, to his joy, that less than an ell remained to go. He dropped onto gravel at the water's edge and called to Ellora to fall. He caught her neatly and held her for a moment close against him. She sighed and turned her face into the curve of his neck. Then he set her feet on the ground, and they turned to look for the cavern that must, they felt sure, be nearby.

The chasm was almost in darkness. Only the tops of the cliffs still burned with sunlight, but that cast enough reflected glow into the deep so they could see the facing walls.

"To the right?" murmured Ellora. They ran their eyes over the rough surfaces, looking for a pool of deeper shadow that would reveal the mouth of the cavern. There was none to be seen. The gravelly beach they stood upon seemed to end at a buttress of rock that thrust its toes into the water at the right end of the beach. The two looked at one another; then they moved toward the outcrop. Nearing it, they looked closely at the surface. Incised into the stone, they saw hand- and foot-holds going round it toward the right.

Johab turned to Ellora. "You are still weak from your long trial and weary from our journey. Wait here, and I will try the handholds and find if they lead to the cavern."

Ellora nodded. "Take care, Johab. We are the last of the Old Lords. The future of our race is within us." Then she smiled and kissed him lightly on the cheek.

He sprang slightly to reach the first of the handholds; his toe found purchase, and he moved easily across the face of the rock and disappeared around its bulk. It seemed very long to the waiting Ellora, but at last he returned to her sight and beckoned. "Come," he cried. "The cavern is here!"

She ran to the buttress and leaped for the holds, as he had done. The way was easy, once she had found the spacing of the holds, and she was with him in less than a hundred heart-beats.

They went together around the stone and dropped to another gravel bar on its other side. There, yawning above them, was the mouth of a tremendous cave, arched and groined like a temple and dark as the entrance to some nether-world.

"There is a stone inside shaped like an arrow. It fits into a slot and turns," said Ellora. They scrambled up the slant of detritus that had collected against the slope and found them-selves standing within that tremendous opening. From her pack, Ellora brought forth a lightglass and turned the wheel that sparked it alight.

The cavern loomed before them, deeper than the little light could penetrate, its walls gleaming with the stuff the Lords called false gold, which glowed clear yellow when the light touched it.

It was empty, save for the moldy carpet of droppings from roosting creatures and piles of rubble that had fallen from the roof through many eons. To their right, once again, there was a smooth slab set into the wall. It seemed natural, yet there was something about it that spoke of hands to the two Lords.

"There is a slot in the stone—see, it looks like a natural crack, just here." She went to the slab and laid her hand in a long fissure. "Where is the stone shaped like an arrow?" she asked. "Can you see it, Johab?"

He was methodically searching among the debris on the floor, sneezing with the dust he made. Ellora moved toward the outer wall of the cavern, looking closely at its surface. Suddenly she caught her breath. Johab stood and came to her side. There, seemingly carven in relief into the wall of the cave, was a stone arrow.

When Johab slipped his fingers about it, it moved, though very slightly. Then the two set about prying it loose, and soon they had it down from the wall.

It was a large thing, half as tall as Ellora, but very thin. Though it had seemed to be stone, it was not. They decided that it must be metal of some sort they had never known existed. It took both of them to guide its awkward length into the slot, for it would only go in at an absolute right angle. Still, they had it in at last and turned it, once more to the right.

There was a moment when nothing happened. Then something grated, and the slab shifted fractionally, one side, the right, moving inward a tiny bit, and the other moving outward.

"It is a pivot stone," said Johab. "That great slab could move no other way, I should think, without many men to winch it up or out. Lend your weight here, Ellora, and we'll have it open."

They laid their shoulders to the slab and heaved. It turned protestingly around, leaving an opening large enough for a man to enter. Then they stopped it with stones, that it might not close until they pleased. The two stood grinning at one another in the dim light of the glass.

"What of the air?" asked Ellora. "It has been many years since this place was shut away."

Johab tore a bit from the tail of his tunic and opened the lightglass, holding the cloth in the center of its spark. The piece smoked, then blazed, and he weighted it with a pebble and tossed it into the opening. It blazed up gaily, then settled down to burn itself out.

The two slipped into the slot and stood in the chamber where their fathers had stored the secrets of their people, in days when such a store seemed wholly unnecessary.

A blaze of reflections and refractions echoed their lightglass. Set into a frame against the wall before them was a tremendous wheel of metal, its thin spokes webbed with filaments that held thousands of crystals, ranging in size from those no greater than the ones in Johab's armband to the diameter of a cartwheel. The greatest was in the center of the thing, the sizes diminishing with their distance from it.

The thing seized the little glow of the glass and turned it into a silent shout of splendor that lit the chamber in echoing ripples of color and sparkle. These were, in turn, caught by other crystal-studded instruments and rebounded, until the two Lords felt themselves to be in the center of a storm of light.

Hurriedly damping the lightglass, Johab said, "The wheel of light—I know of it, Ellora. Its place is in my father's wall. He told me of it when I was too young to realize its power and use, but I remember. It must be set into the frame made for it, that it may use the sun's light by day and the triple moons' by night. That frame must still exist, for the walls my fathers built were not meant to be razed by such lazy folk as these usurpers. We must take these things, all of them, across the plain to the place of Juthar, where Enthala stood near the city of Golath."

"Then we shall do it," said Ellora. "The folk are skilled and willing. The gods are guiding us. Let us go out and up and tell our people that we hold in our hands the key to victory."

They looked about them again. Light still danced and glanced and sparkled from every wall, from racks of crystal-studded things upon the floor, and most of all from the Great Wheel, whose concentric web of glory shimmered unbearably. But the light was beginning to dim, with the quenching of the lightglass, and one by one the lesser crystals winked out.

The Lords turned to their entrance, slipped through. But Ellora put her head through once more to gaze upon the long-forgotten storehouse. Her breath caught in her throat, and she tugged at Johab's sleeve as she drew him back to the slot.

"See, Johab! Look at the Great Wheel!"

Johab peered into the chamber. All was again in darkness . . . almost. But at the center of the Wheel, where the giant crystal was hung, there was a sullen eye of red, blazing steadily into the darkness.

The Wheel was awake and alive once again, and only untold years of night could put it back to sleep.

12

The Labor in the Deep

NONE but the Lords might again have made their way up the perilous path to that apron of rock where the folk waited. Night had wiped away all the golden light. The triple moons spun at an angle that hid their glow from the depths of the Chasm of Genlith. Only the Lords' sharply honed gifts of seeing without eyes enabled them to find their holds upon the cliffside.

As they neared their goal, they could see the comforting redness of flame. They knew that the people had made ready for their return, and it gave them new strength. Climbing the last spans, they smelled the food prepared for the night meal and exerted themselves to reach that grateful spot where it waited.

Ruthan watched above. Her hand was extended into the shadow to help Ellora over the last yard. Then Johab was swung up, and the group stood together, feeling the triumphant mood of the Lords envelop them.

Johab and Ellora joined hands, and Johab said, "The tools of our people lie below, as we were promised. The work of raising them will be awesome, but we are all strong and fit. It will be done. Give gratitude to the gods, plains-children.

We have in our hands the weapons to free our lands of the usurpers."

A murmur rose from the assembled people. They smiled, and their eyes shone in the firelight. Jearth laid his hand upon Johab's shoulder and said, "Truly, all our journey is made worthwhile. Now we must rest and eat and grow strong, for the task is just beginning. Come to the fire, Lords, and take food with us."

They slept that night in a strange sort of security of spirit, fearing no enemy's approach, no untoward thing. They felt the hands of the gods working about them and no uneasy qualm disturbed their rest. But the first light that touched the crags above them and outlined the spire to the east with gold-on-black found them waking. They rose as one and went hurriedly about the preparations for the task ahead.

The morning meal was soon dispatched, and all was made ready for descent into the deeps. Those who faced the downward climb were warned of every pitfall on the way, while those who were to remain above were set to making a heavy frame of tree trunks to hold a windlass, with which they hoped to raise the weapons from their long resting place.

Johab secured one of their painfully transported cables to the skeleton of the frame and was lowered over the precipice directly above the cavern's mouth. In this manner he hoped to be able to avoid the time-consuming climb into the chasm. But the cave mouth was deeply overhung with rock. The line went downward, directly to the swift, cold river, and only his tugs and cries kept him from a wetting among the tumbled rocks amid the waters.

"None of us may descend by that route," he gasped as he clambered again onto the apron of rock. "Even if we secured the line above and below, the spray from the river makes all slippery. There is too much danger that someone might miss a handhold on the rope and plunge into the stream. While we may be willing to die in aid of the gods' purposes, I do not propose to waste even one person's life."

"What of raising the crystals by that way?" asked Ellora, vigorously rubbing his wet head with a rough bit of cloth. "It would seem that we might make framework to keep them from swinging into the rock face. It would be nearly impossible to bring them up that path for grasshoppers, not to mention how we might bring them across the buttress that extends into the river."

"Some such way must be devised," Johab answered, rescuing his tousled hair from her ministrations. "We must go down and see the place by day. We must test the weight of the different pieces and consider how best we may raise them. They were put into that place by our fathers, and what our fathers could lower, we can surely bring up again!"

So the Lords again went down to the bottom of the chasm, and their people followed cautiously in their track. Those above, directed by Ruthan and Jearth, made all ready for the terrible task of lifting the strange weapons again to the light of day.

The chasm was a different place in the light of a clear morning. The river hissed madly among the rocks in its bed, casting mists of rainbow into the sunlight. The rocks themselves, it seemed, were molded of clear yellow light and seemed insubstantial as sunbeams. The handholds on the buttress were etched in black shadow on that yellow stone, and no one had difficulty in seeing the way in which they must go. Swiftly they followed the Lords, and long before the sun reached deeply into the canyon they stood within the cavern.

Ellora again laid her hand to the key on the rock wall. Johab helped her to align it with the slot and to turn it. The plainsfolk gasped as the slab shifted, but soon they lent their strength toward opening it wide for the first time in many years. They chose large stones to hold it in place, and the opening thus revealed was broad enough for six men to stand within it, side by side.

The darkness in the storehouse was lit by one red eye of light, and the Lords turned to the people. "Our lightglass, when we stood here before, lit the great crystal in the center of the wheel to life. You can see that it still glows. The power is there, ready to our hands, but I must caution you. These devices use not only the powers of light but also those of thought. Anger may find itself magnified a hundredfold and reflected upon its originator. We must guard ourselves against any evil thing inside us, harness our spirits as well as our bodies to our work. Dangerous thinking can make its own death, when you deal with such things as the Great Wheel of Arthoa."

There was a murmur from the folk, and their eyes turned to that sullen gleam that seemed to stare back at them knowingly.

"Lord," said Huthear, the Eldest of these folk, "we shall take care. But is there danger to those who lay hands upon these things? We are not learned in things of power, and we may be awkward in their handling."

"We will be with you, directing every move," said Ellora. "There can be danger to those who know nothing of the weapons. But while we had never seen them, we were trained, nevertheless, in their uses and their care. We know the ways of those who made them. We understand the forces that stimulate them. We will safeguard you."

She went into the chamber. Her hands moved among the lesser weapons and drew forth a small triangular frame strung with diamond-shaped crystals that were cut, each one, into thousands of facets. When she moved it, the light that found its way into the chamber from the lightglasses in the cavern was broken into infinities of tiny ripples of brightness that danced on the walls and the floor.

"It would be well to leave the lightglasses there," she called to Johab. "This rhythyl will use their little glow to give us worklight. Its gleaming will not excite any of the great weapons or the Wheel. It will be safer to move it in its nearly dormant state, and the other weapons will not derive power from it as we handle them."

Then Johab and the people also came into the chamber and set their hands to the smaller weapons. None of those except the rhythyl was small enough to carry in one hand, for the crystals that hung from them in all shapes and sizes were cut of dense stuff, heavy to the hand, even in a palm-sized crystal.

By midafternoon they had moved all the lesser devices into the cavern, arranged them by weight and bulk and had secured lines over the lip of the precipice from above to attempt raising them. But the Great Wheel still stood in the chamber, and it was with caution that the Lords approached it. Only Huthear and his son Thearon were allowed to aid them, and the four stationed themselves evenly across the chamber, moving toward the thing from different directions at an even pace. They arrived together and laid their hands upon it simultaneously.

Their palms tingled. The hair rose on their necks, and they felt within their bones a deep *thrumm* of vibration that echoed along their nerves for many heartbeats. The plainsfolk turned uneasy eyes upon the two Lords. Ellora and Johab stood still, hands upon the Wheel, eyes closed, focusing the strength of their wills and spirits upon the terrible thing they sought to master.

For a long time they stood, locked in their silent struggle. Huthear and his son closed their eyes and held their spirits in stillness, their bodies in acquiescence, knowing that any incautious move or thought might work the deaths of the Lords. With the tough acceptance of their people, they held fast. The time seemed very long.

At last the Lords opened their eyes and turned them toward one another.

"It is stilled," said Ellora, "as much as it can be when it is no longer asleep."

Johab nodded and raised his hands from the frame of the Wheel. "We may move it now," he said to Huthear. "We have, I believe, tuned it to our wills, and that was no small task. Our fathers were older and stronger and better trained than we. They and their own fathers and their father's fathers made this thing, and it was attuned to their wills."

The four set their hands again to the framework and drew the Wheel forth from the wall. Behind it stood a wheeled cart that seemed made for bearing its shape and weight. As two tilted the thing forward, the others slipped the carrier beneath the curve at its bottom. It settled into place easily, held by metal brackets that snapped about it, and was borne up to clear the floor by the straightening-up of the trolleylike cart.

When they began to roll it across the floor of the chamber, the crystals began to hum, softly at first, then more loudly and intensely as the vibration continued. Warned, the Lords halted until there was again quiet in the chamber. Then, a few steps at a time, stopping between, they carefully moved it from the chamber and into the cavern, placing it at the end of the line of things of great weight.

"This is the key, the magnifier, the source of power for the rest of the weapons. It must go last, and it must not be lost. Many of the others, while useful, are not of terrible importance. But the Wheel would be the one thing we must have, if we were forced to choose among the many things here. We must perfect our way of raising the other weapons before we trust this to our system," Ellora said, as they settled it into place.

Now the sun was again lost behind the crags to the west, leaving only its last rays on the peaks to light the gorge. Those in the cavern were unwilling to kindle lightglasses, for the Wheel glowered into the gathering darkness with its terrible eye, and they had no liking for disturbing it further. Making certain that each of the devices was securely set and braced against falling, they made ready to ascend the cliff before the light was gone.

The Lords came last, watching those before them, guiding them with shouts, if they seemed likely to veer from the tested way. Behind, the gorge sank into purple shadow, then to blackness. Ellora, looking back into the deep, saw against the farther wall of the gorge a glow of red pouring from the cavern-mouth and knew that the Wheel was growing in power, even with all the care they had taken.

That night moved slowly. Lords and folk alike were kindled with purpose and excitement, ready to go forward with the work at hand. So first light saw all ready to begin again. No time was lost in making ready the frames that had been prepared to hold the ropes and their precious freight clear of the overhang. While Johab was hanging on the lines, making them fast, Ellora was going among the folk gathering spare clothing, bedding, anything soft and suitable for wrapping the crystals.

When they stood again in the Cavern of Genlith, the Lords went at once to the Wheel, which stood glowing and, again, humming with power that it was gathering from the dimly filtered light coming from the cave mouth. Swiftly they began to wrap the crystals securely, beginning with those at the edges of the frame. As they worked inward, the hum dimmed, the glow quieted. When they came to the crystal in the center, it was with trepidation that they laid the cloth across its width and stepped back to judge the effect of the muffling.

Angrily, the crystal pulsed red, its glow penetrating the cloth. The Lords laid more layerings over it until no light could be seen. Then they tied down the wrappings so tightly that handling would not loosen them. The Wheel was as safe as it could be made in the present circumstances.

The time had come to attempt raising the first of the weapons. The rhythyl, lightest of all, went up easily, fended from the rock by the frames and by a guiding pole. Encouraged, the Lords made the lines fast about a second device, a single crystal cut in diamond shape with only eight facets. It was as tall as Johab, set into a heavy frame of metal, and its weight was a very different thing from that of the rhythyl.

When those above, signaled by a tug on the line, set their strength against the ropes, the weapon moved sluggishly from the gravel of the river bank. Those below lifted as long as they could reach it. Then they thrust upward with their poles to control its tendency to swing inward. As it came near the overhang, some peculiarity of its weight and shape made it swing close beneath the frame, as if it sought to smash itself against the rock. Frantic cries brought the pullers to a halt, and Johab stood beside Ellora, gazing upward in thought.

"We must bring down the rhythyl again," Ellora said, at last. "I know something of its uses, for my father possessed one, and I was instructed in its functions. It can be made to help us."

So the rhythyl was let down on a light line and hung over the river in a storm of quivering light. It was quickly hooked with a pole and brought to hand. Ellora moved backward and forward, studying the angle of the sunlight, holding the rhythyl at different angles, casting its refractions against the rock above.

At last, she took position. "Johab, will you aid me?" she asked. "We must keep the light of the rhythyl against the weapon as if it were a pole, while with our wills we push it outward to miss the overhang. It is no small task, for one of us must divide his attention, keeping the light focused. Still, it can be done."

And it was done; while the folk strained at ropes and poles, the Lords strained at more tenuous things. The shining crystal rose, unimpeded, until it reached the upper frame, where it was secured by those above, who quickly lifted it to the safety of the apron of rock on which they stood.

Now the work went swiftly. Those above raised piece after piece of the strange weaponry, aided by the guiding poles or the beams of the rhythyl. The morning passed, and the afternoon was half-spent when they halted their exertions.

"We need not drive ourselves to exhaustion," said Johab. "There is time to rest and to work, also. Let us take our rest, now, and we shall be the fresher in the morning."

So the workers returned to the camping-place, and food and rest soon raised their spirits. The two Lords sat apart, however, and spoke in hushed tones.

"I feel a moving in the air," whispered Ellora, and her eyes turned toward the hold of Mirreh. "There is something afoot among our enemies, and I fear for all the common folk who remain uncorrupted by their treacheries.

"It has come to me, Johab, that we must plant the seeds of its destruction at the roots of Olanthe. There is among the devices in the cavern one whose crystal may serve our cause. Taken from its frame, it may be carried, with effort, by a single person. It can be made to amplify vibration and thought. I know the one spot beneath the cliff on which Olanthe stands where untoward vibration may bring the city toppling from its height."

"I also know of the carthol," said Johab. "Its crystal would serve us well, used so. However, there is no necessity for anyone to stay behind to trigger its resonances. When the Great Wheel is set into its frame, it can focus our thought upon the hidden crystal. With the vibrations set up at that time, we will be able to bring many catastrophes at once against our enemies."

The sun sank behind the mountains, and the Lords and

their folk went to their sleep, but in the minds of the Lords there moved portents of fear and suffering, echoes of despair. Their rest was broken and fitful.

When light again rode in the east, they were up and preparing food for the sleepers. Before the sun was well up all were in the deeps once more, and the weapons were rising, one by one, from their long rest.

On the third day there was nothing left to bring up except the Great Wheel of Arthoa. It stood with its crystals wrapped, but nevertheless it hummed with an almost inaudible flow of power that one could feel thrumming through his bones, if he stood nearby.

The Lords, with Huthear and Thearon, moved it slowly to the cave mouth. Lines were made fast about its frame, and it was swung easily outward until it stood on the gravel bar under the overhang. The sun struck it fully, and those who tended it felt the hair rise upon their heads, their flesh gather into ridges at the potential that gathered about it.

Johab leaped for a line and clambered swiftly upward to the camping-place. In a moment, he was letting himself down again, and they held the poles ready to hook him to shore. About his shoulders he had bound heavy blankets, and Ellora loosed them from him as quickly as she could. Then they draped and bound the thick stuff about the Wheel, swaddling it away from the sun. The quiver died out of the air, and their hair lay smooth again.

Many lines were secured to the Wheel. Those above crawled out onto the frames in order to guide the lines and the Wheel with more control. Ellora and Johab manned the rhythyl, and Huthear stood apart and prayed to the gods, as the terrible thing began its ascent.

It swung, dark and dangerous, moving in slow circles as it rose up the cliff. The beams of the rhythyl nudged it gently this way and that, as it came too near projections of stone. Even that rippling light could not brighten its aspect. The folk labored, the sun shone, the Lords willed, the Wheel moved. It was as though time had set itself to extend this moment indefinitely into the future; as though there would never be an end.

But the Wheel stood at last upon the rock above, and the Lords joined hands and faced their people.

"Now we must let our ways part for a time," said Johab. "Most must come with me, bearing these things back to Enthala, my father's house, where the frame stands that will make the Wheel workable for us. But Ellora must go, taking with her a crystal to place beneath the city of Olanthe. Who will go with her?"

Ellora shook her head. "No one must go with me. I went forth alone, so they believe. If I am taken, I must still be alone. Let only your prayers go with me. And make haste. There is death on the wind."

13

At the Roots of Olanthe

ELLORA stood on the road, looking after the last of her people as they toiled from sight around the bend. She did not raise her hand, nor did she call out. She turned at last and followed the road that curled around the shoulder of the mountain. Further on, she knew, there was a path that led up and over the top of the ridge, saving many a weary mile of walking in the cart-track. She knew that, with great effort, she could use the animal trails across the backs of the ridges that lay between this spot and Olanthe.

On her back, wrapped snugly in her own blanket, was the large crystal from the carthol. Its weight was a third of her own, and she weighed it in the balance of her judgment as she considered her course. With the past weeks of good food and hard work, she had come again to the fitness of body that she had known before her stay in the dungeons of Mirreh. The orange sun warmed her face and shoulders with its kindly rays, and the air of the mountains was crisp and strengthening. Never had she felt more apt for effort. She would walk the ridges. Even that way the journey would be slow, but it would be safest.

Before the sun had run its course across the sky, she had mounted to the top of the eminence against which the road lay. Far below, too far for vision, lay the Chasm of Genlith. Away to the north and west, so her inner vision told her, moved Johab and the plainsfolk. To the south, beyond further, higher ridges, lay Olanthe. She smiled and looked about for shelter for the night.

A niche in the rock of the mountain hid her small fire and provided a place for her to spread her blanket. She made her meal in the flickering glow of the blaze; then she turned to the unwrapped crystal that she had leaned against a boss of rock.

Focusing her attention upon it, she visualized the cavern of Genlith. She created, in her thought, a vibration that carried down through the stone upon which the crystal stood to the depths of the mountain. She saw inside her skull the shaking of old dust within the cavern, the tinkling collapse of stalactites, the quivering of the walls. She brought down the cavern in a moil of dust and stone.

The firelight gleamed with a cold green flame in the center of the crystal. It grew in intensity as her thought fed into it. The triple moons rode up the sky, and the crystal burned with terrible fires, the facets gleaming green. The rock began to vibrate. In the depths of the mountain there was a grinding and groaning. The bushes danced a weird pavane, then stilled. Ellora closed her eyes and sent her spirit down to the cavern mouth far below. But there was no cave there. Only a tumble of rubble that might have fallen yesterday or a thousand years ago marked the spot.

She smiled. Her thought again went out, over long miles. "Johab," she said to him, "the crystal does its work. I have collapsed the cavern. No mischance of fate may take our enemies there to uncover our workings. Take heart!"

Johab's answering thought came. "It is well done. Take care, Ellora, for my heart is empty without your presence."

The Lord Ellora smiled into the firelight. "I see something of the future, Johab," she murmured, "and it will be long before I look on you again. Hold me in heart!" But she did not send that message across the sundering miles.

When the sun again warmed the peaks to westward, she was on her way, the weight of the crystal between her shoulder blades. The way was steep and rough, and she found that the added weight affected her balance, as well as her judgment of the effort required, when she must leap or carry her own weight by her hands. Still she persisted, and after a time there came into her body a sort of rhythm that carried her through the long days that followed.

The only breaks in that rhythm came when her sensing told her of men and women—shepherds of the mountain herds or hunters or gatherers of herbs and fuel—who might intersect her path or see her as she moved. At such times she dropped into crevices or thickets and waited until no spark of sentience touched her probing spirit. Yet there came a day when one of these called upon her with a cry she could not resist.

The afternoon was waning, and Ellora was descending a difficult stretch of scree, testing her footing, balancing the crystal precariously as she labored. In the midst of the effort, she was caught in a wash of pain and fear that nearly sent her to her knees. Pausing, she felt outward . . . and found below her an entity trapped where she had fallen among rocks.

Ellora stood in the sunglare, her face turned southward. So much depended upon the successful placing of the crystal. So much depended upon the usurpers' belief in their own safety, until the very end. And yet . . . it was contrary to everything her people had been and taught to pass by a being in pain and trouble. She sent a desperate query into the spaces . . . "Johab, will I imperil you if I go to the aid of one who suffers?"

On the returning wind, his reply . . . "Our people do not work in the ways of the usurpers. If the gods send our ends upon the injury of a worker in the mountains, so be it."

So she turned again to her task and found her way down to

a path that wound near to the place where she sensed the presence of the injured shepherd, who lay in silent desperation, waiting for death. Down a tumble of rocks and scrub, through a maze of boulders she went and turned her steps into a cul-de-sac. There she saw the crumpled body of the shepherd girl, wedged into a V of rock.

"My sister," she called softly, "help is at hand."

The girl moved a hand, tried to turn her head. "I am tightly caught. My arm is broken, I think. None can help me from this place unaided. But my thanks for your presence. It will ease my dying."

"Who are you who has no hope?" asked Ellora. "The folk of Lord Jornaval have never been so accepting of catastrophes without any struggle against them!"

"When we were his folk, we had hope," whispered the girl. "Now we are the slaves of Mirreh, overseen by his scourgers. Care and loyalty for one another is punished by whipping, or by death. No one will be allowed to search for me, when I do not return with the sheep at nightfall. My own people will know that I am hurt or dead, but they will not seek after me. The tale-bearers would report them to the scourgers, and they would be mutilated or killed. It happened to me so. I was whipped skinless for searching for my own man. My mother nursed me in secret, else the same would have happened to her. And though I found him, I could not save him, for he was dead. I shall soon be with him."

"But if no one searches, why do your people not slip away into the plain or the hills?" Ellora asked.

"None is allowed to go down the mountain. Only up it with herds or flocks or equipment for harvesting herbs. All possible ways are watched. And those few who have fled left behind families who were tortured slowly to death as a lessoning to the rest. Be certain, we cannot escape in good conscience."

Ellora unslung her pack and unwrapped the crystal.

"My sister, would you relish revenge against Mirreh?" she asked. "I can free you. I give you my name, and with it my life, should you betray me. I am Ellora, daughter to Jornaval, bearer of destruction upon Olanthe and Mirreh, if the gods hold me in their hands."

"I am Gertra, once wife to Olnar, now shepherd of the Tarniel Clan. Revenge is the one thing that might stay my feet from the path my love has walked before me. Freed, I will aid you in all ways that I can, Lord Ellora."

The crystal was turned to catch the long slant of sun rays that fell across the breast of the mountain. Ellora thought into it a quiet tremor, a mere shiver of atoms. The green fire sparked into life, but dimly. The rock shimmered, and a thin dust rose. Then the great boulder that wedged Gertra's head and shoulders against her knees shivered and broke into pebbles. Ellora was there to catch the woman in her arms, cradling her against further injury.

The broken arm was soon set; food and water brought color back into the girl's pale face. Knowing that none would seek for her, they made themselves free of the mountain, and a good fire was fed through the night to aid her recovery from the shock of the fall.

In the light of morning they set out together toward Olanthe, and Gertra marched step for step with Ellora, never complaining of the pain of her broken arm. With a companion to help with the precious crystal in steep places, Ellora found her speed greatly increased.

She informed Johab of this when they were once again settled for the night. "Make haste," she said to him, across the leagues. "I will come to Olanthe in three days, if no untoward thing happens to me. Make haste across the plain, Johab!"

His whispered answer came across the ways. "We lie far out upon the plain. Tomorrow will see us well on the way for,

93

laden though we are with our great burdens, we have made speed. Take care, Ellora. Come safely to Olanthe . . . and also back to me."

There was need for care as the two women drew nearer to the city. There were many about the tracks and trails that scarred the mountains, and Ellora knew that the time must come when they must travel among other wayfarers, hoping that none might know them to be different from the peasant folk whose business took them to the city. So they wrapped the crystal of the carthol with the blanket and the supplies, making it look like a pack of goods to be sold at market. They rearranged their clothing as best they could, that they might resemble the other country people who approached the city of Olanthe.

Gertra gave Ellora her head scarf, making it into a coïf that overhung her brow, hiding her eyes, for they knew that anyone who had ever met one of the Lords must recognize those piercing and farseeing eyes without fail. Word of one possessing such eyes would go swiftly to Mirreh.

Now they drew near, indeed, to their goal. The paths were roads, and the roads highways, all thronged with people going and coming, laden with burdens. None laughed aloud, none smiled or joked, as they had in the old days. A grimness had settled over the land, and the people endured, but they did not smile at strangers or ask them where they fared.

In the forenoon of the third day, they rounded a curve in their road and saw Olanthe rising before them, its graceful curves of wall and structure, its restful cream-colored roofs glowing gold in the light of the orange sun. Ellora caught Gertra's hand and stopped.

"There is pain in my heart," she said, "when I think of destroying this lovely thing that my fathers made. Olanthe crowns the crag with loveliness. What a pity to pull it down into rubble and dust!"

"It is the face of a lovely woman who hides a foul heart,"

answered Gertra. "You dwelt for very long in the dungeon beneath its cellars. While you were hidden away in the darkness, Mirreh made changes in the people who lived in the city. Those who thought their own thoughts were killed or driven away. Many people were brought from the plains city of Golath, and they were given the houses and the shops of those who were gone. They are sheep-folk, not of our kind. Only the mindless and heartless of our own people stayed within the walls of Olanthe.

"Some of the exiles came to us in the far heights, telling us of the works of Mirreh. When those with scourges came to rule over us in the name of Mirreh, we pretended that those exiles were our own people, and so we saved them. One of them was Olnar, my husband. He said to me that Olanthe should be wiped from the land, so false and spiritless is the life led within it now. We do well, Lord, to rid our land of it, and of Mirreh and those who dwell where those who were better than they built."

Ellora was comforted. Raising her burden again to her shoulders, she set forth down the road. But she took care not to look again at the lovely shape of Olanthe, growing larger and brighter as they approached.

A half-league or so from the gates, she turned aside from the road into a narrow track that wound down the slope of the mountainside. Beside an outcrop of stone crowned by trailing vines and ferns she stopped as if to rest, allowing an approaching traveler to pass by on his way up to the road. Then, beckoning to Gertra, she slipped from view as though she had been swallowed up. But Gertra followed closely, and they found themselves in a slitlike place that wound down the slope between walls of split and fractured rock that twisted, mazelike, with many choices of path and direction. Ellora knew her way and chose truly, never finding herself in doubt, never needing to search for a guiding sign.

"This was one of my play-places when I was a child," she

murmured to Gertra. "None I ever knew seemed to know of it. Likely no one but an exploring child would have had the time or taken the pains to search out a way through this tumble to find where it led. How strangely the gods lay out their patterns. Now it will help us to save our people from their enslavers."

The maze trail dropped swiftly, forcing them to move with care for the crystal. After a long time it ended upon the edge of a cliff, leaving them to face a precarious stairway of fallen boulders that leaned out into the gulf below. It was well that Gertra was there, even though she had only one hand with which to help, for Ellora found that she must climb down, leaving the crystal behind; then Gertra could let it down to her by the strong line from her pack. In this way, they made their way down the slope more quickly than one alone could have managed. At the bottom they found themselves in the cleft of a stream that gushed out from the rock on which sat the city of Olanthe.

"There is a cavern with room to walk beside the water," said Ellora. "I must go into it and set the crystal, but it is perilous, Gertra. Mirreh may have set guards there, and I must go quietly, able to hide myself at any moment.

"I need one who will go to Johab, if need be, to tell him that our task is done. I have no time, now, to send my spirit seeking his. I feel the compulsion of the gods, and I must hurry to set the crystal in its place. Go back to the road, Gertra, climbing always to the left, except where I have set a mark on the rock. Wait in a safe place, and I will send my thought to you, when the thing is done. Then if I do not return, go to Johab in the plain. When there is time, I will touch my thought to his and tell him that you are coming."

Gertra did not question. She embraced Ellora, stepped back, and raised her hand. "I will go to the plain, Lord; but I well know that you send me for my own safety. Go with the gods,

Lord." She turned and began the rough climb toward the maze.

Ellora watched her for a short moment, a half-smile upon her lips. Then she gazed attentively up and down the cleft of the gorge. In the very heart of his stronghold though it might be, Mirreh surely would have set guards here . . . unless it had never occurred to his limited mind that a city set over a fracture in the rock might easily be brought down. Mirreh's kind had no knowledge of the ways in which it might be done. However it was, she could see no guards, hear no footfall, catch no hint of human thought in the length of the gorge. Though there was some evidence in footprints and bits of gear that men of some sort did come here.

So she moved swiftly into the mouth of the cavern that bored into the cliff. Soon she found it necessary to kindle her lightglass, for the twisting of the tunnel shut off the light. Then she felt truly alone, with only the hushed *susurru* of the water for company.

Her lightglass beam crisscrossed the walls of the tunnel, searching for the betraying shadow that would show the mouth of the fracture she sought. There, yes, there it was, a dark line against the umber of the rock wall. With soundless speed, she covered the distance and slipped into the fissure. It was narrow, and she found that she must remove her pack in order to negotiate it. She clasped the precious bundle in her arms and slithered deeper into the crack, bending sidewise, backward, sometimes almost double, but pursuing it until she could move no deeper.

She dropped to her knees in the widest spot she could find and unwrapped the carthol crystal. Laying it against the wall as nearly upright as the unevenness would permit, she wedged it fast with loose stones. Then she sat before it and closed her eyes, pouring all the strength of will she had into the command that she fed into the waiting device. The green glow wakened the crystal, and a quiver of power rippled across its surface. The air shimmered with potential. Little veils of dust shook down from the walls. Ellora sat still, willing into the carthol the commands upon which she and Johab had decided.

At last she opened her eyes. The quiver in the air and the rock had subsided, the dust settled. Only the green eye at the center of the carthol crystal remained, glowing evilly from the wall of the cleft. It waited, now, for a touch, a thought, a sending from afar to set it vibrating.

Wearily, Ellora leaned against the wall. She turned her thought to Gertra, waiting above. "It is done!" she cried in her mind. "Go now, for I feel the approach of many men. I must cover my trail, so that they will not suspect what I have done. Go to Johab in the plain and tell him that I will join him when I may."

Then she hurried from the chamber and the fissure, wrapping her bundle together and hiding it in a crack near the mouth of the tunnel.

Swiftly, she moved in the darkness, for her lightglass was left behind with all the betraying things the plains people had given her. Feeling before her with her other senses, marking the approach of the men, she failed to attend closely to her footing. A round stone betrayed her, sending her headlong into unconsciousness.

14

Journey to Enthala

THE orange sun stood low above the plain, waning westward. Johab walked among his folk, lending his strength where it might be needed, as they wearied beneath the burdens they bore. Yet his heart always yearned toward the southern mountains, and his will alone kept his seeing spirit attuned to his abreet as it circled, seeking always for danger.

The leagues they had covered were a soreness in their bones and a weariness in their memories. Still, none slackened pace or cried out for rest. When the sun went below the horizon, then they would stop at the first grove for rest and food. Now all walked automatically, neither feeling nor thinking. Except for Johab.

At midafternoon, he had heard in his soul the cry that Ellora had sent to Gertra, though only by his honed spirit could such a short and distant communication have been heard. He knew that her task was done, and knowing this, he longed to cry out to her. But he knew that this would leave his people open to danger, without the eyes of his spirit keeping watch for them. So he longed for the night when he could again relax his burdened heart and seek for her in the south.

When the sun was gone and a copse loomed dimly in their path, there was great relief in the hearts of all. Johab rejoiced, made his meal quickly, and composed himself to seek south-ward. When he was ready, he sent his thought forth from his body gladly . . . but he found no answering spirit to receive him. Through the distance he cried, "Ellora!" but there was no reply.

Then he thought of the companion whom she had taken from the rocks, and he turned his mind to Gertra. This was a difficult thing, for she had no training in the gifts of the mind, and only the undeveloped aptitude that lay in her people. Only her close association with Ellora and her utter willingness allowed her, at last, to find his voice speaking in her mind. Though in her earlier life she would have feared such a thing, now she did not. She had looked upon death and found it a friend. She had given her service into the hands of the gods. So she held her spirit open to Johab, and he spoke to her, and she answered.

When he had learned what she had to tell, he took thought. Then he said, "Though Ellora sent you to me, there is another task you might do to serve a greater purpose. Your people, the Tarniel . . . I see in your thought that they mislike the new ruler and fear him. Is there one among them who could lead them, at need? One whom they would trust and follow without question? One who also knows and trusts you?"

"My grandfather, Otor, is such a one," the girl answered. "He was eldest of our clan, our leader, until the scourgers came. Then he was driven from the village into the mountains. He has lived because he was the ablest, as well as the eldest. His love for our folk is matched only by his enmity toward Mirreh. The people talk with him when they go into the heights for wood and to seek after straying beasts. They share with him from their stores, though each measure is counted by the new rulers, and they must take what they give him from their own mouths."

"Can you walk again to the mountaintop and find your grandsire?" asked Johab. "Can you tell him to hold himself in readiness to lead his people again . . . against their oppressors?"

"I can, and I will," said Gertra. "I knew that the Lord Ellora sent me to you for my own safety. I would rather work than flee. Give me your message, and I will take it to my grandfather. I will hide with him until the time comes to move against the scourgers."

Johab set into her mind the message for Otor, though it seemed strange to him to be commanding an Elder, one whom he did not know. It was in some way, to his mind, pretentious for one of his tender age, even though he was a Lord, in all truth, to direct those so much older and, in many ways, wiser than he. Yet when it was done he felt much eased in his mind. He had forewarned and guided at least one small part of the people who were Ellora's folk. He returned to his place and slept, though his unease at Ellora's silence troubled his rest, and he rose early in the morning and made the meal for the plainspeople before they waked.

They had been untroubled by a hint of danger for so long, since their first arrival in the mountains, that the purring cry of their abreet brought them up short with surprise. It swooped from its high circling near midday, and Johab set his mind's eye within the creature and took it aloft again, scanning the plain and the horizon with close attention.

The plain stretched in its copse-dotted expanse for league after league to east, to west, to north. He extended his range, circling further afield, and then his sensors caught the thing that had disturbed the abreet. Men moved upon the plain to the west, their number strung out in a line that pointed toward the southern slopes.

He brought the abreet lower, still at a great distance, and brought its eye-cells to full magnification. Forty men and women moved in that distant line. All bore burdens, though many pack-beasts followed behind. At the head of the line rode men upon crawlers, and the standard that flashed with gold and scarlet behind them told Johab that these were the folk of his enemies. So . . . the usurpers moved together upon the gameboard.

Low and swiftly, he brought the abreet away from the marchers. Then he returned to himself and turned to his folk. "Golath is upon the plain. I believe he moves with his troops and his slaves, together with men of Mirreh's force. There are many troops and forty of the city people, as well as beasts of burden. We must turn from our direct way, for we must not meet them here. We must again take cover and travel by night, for the abreet from Olanthe may come to meet them and could see us upon the plain. Our days of carefree travel are over."

They turned aside into the first copse and covered their tracks, though there were few of those. The weather was now dry, and the soil was iron-hard and did not scar easily. They passed the rest of the day resting but watchful, and when the sun sank below the horizon's rim they moved with the darkness onto the plain.

To the west, on the very edge of perception, they saw a glare against the sky that told of campfires of men who felt themselves safe and unwatched. The triple moons spun, their light clean and cold and comforting, but the red smear against the western sky lent the people caution and speed. None who did not know the plainsfolk would have believed the distance they covered before the sun again cast its forerunners of light into the east.

When their abreet again went aloft they were resting in a grove. The device turned westward, and Johab's gaze once again swept the plain in search of their enemies. Those were again on the march, driving the unlucky townsfolk as if they were cattle. They moved southward, still, over the hot plain, and their line of march had angled toward that which his own people pursued. By midday, at the pace the enemy was holding, the group would be near the copse in which he now lay.

He knew that at midday the blazing heat of that orange sun would make the cool purple shadows under the leatherwoods look dangerously inviting. The self-indulgent men he had known while he lay in the metal cells would never hold themselves to their disagreeable task when ease and coolness lay so near.

Johab opened his eyes and looked into those of Ruthan. "We must move from this place," he said. "Those who march will come too near. We must be hidden, and there is no other grove of leatherwood nearby."

The girl smiled and called softly to her husband.

Jearth came quietly and knelt beside them. Ruthan took his hand and said, "Tell the Lord of our newly learned craft, which we found it necessary to devise when the usurpers sought to subdue us."

Jearth chuckled. "Indeed, Lord, we have learned to disappear!"

Johab straightened his back and sat up suddenly. "To disappear, Jearth? This is a thing that even my own people never accomplished, except by actually going to another place altogether."

The man laughed aloud. "This is no thing of great art or high craft; though indeed, it is no small thing, either. We dress, as you have seen but perhaps not truly noticed, in cloth the color of the soil and the dried grasses. We bear, each of us, in our bedding rolls bits of rough matting. Given but a few seconds of warning, we can sink to the ground, scuff out a sort of hollow, cover ourselves with the matting, and look like the plain itself. It is no comfortable thing, even by night. In the day we have often felt that we would never come alive from beneath the mats. But we have always survived. The thing can be done, even at midday."

Johab smiled. "My fathers did well to choose the people of the plain for their own folk. We shall go out as far as can be done in the time left to us and dig into the stuff of the plain, hiding that which we carry as well as ourselves. Your craft may well mean the success of our task."

When the people of Golath and Mirreh came near the inviting copse, it was empty of life and of any sign that men had ever taken shelter there. The plain all about it was empty, too, rolling horizonward on every hand as though no beings but they existed upon it. With pleasure they took their ease there, neglecting their duty to go forward. Even Golath himself saw no need to forward his cause at the expense of his comfort.

Out on the plain, sweltering beneath the matting, choking in the dust stirred by any smallest movement, the plains people lay about Johab. That Lord lay very still, for his seeing spirit went among the trees toward his enemy Golath. This was perilous, for even one who lacked the far-seeing gift that the Lords had in such abundance might possibly feel the touch of another mind upon his own. Only the most delicate of probes might go undetected; only the most subtle questing might fail to rouse the spirit's wardens to its defense.

Lightly as a sun ray falling on a leaf, Johab let his seeing alight within his prey. Golath sprawled upon a bed-pad in the deepest shade, sucking on a wine flask. His men kept better order, directing the slaves and seeing to the beasts, but Johab paid no attention to the bustle about him. He moved, gently, gently, gently, toward the spark that was the innermost self of Golath, settling into that wine-befuddled brain with the inconsequence of a random thought.

In all his long captivity, he had not tried to read his captor. He had avoided that wicked mind, in his own defense. Now he found himself in ill company, for the dark passages that surrounded him were full of evil things. Even the forefront of that miserable mind was tenanted by diseased images and warped impulses. Still, the information he sought was there, also, and he confirmed his belief that Golath was moving toward Olanthe, there to confront/join forces with/confound

/outwit Mirreh. The legions of lies that he had told to excuse his loss of the captive Johab danced dimly about the edges of his memory. More clearly, the suspicion-become-a-certainty that Mirreh was likewise concealing something from him marched across the forefront of his thought. His spies had been silent, which filled his devious mind with speculations.

More than all, though, there was the conviction that the mechanisms that Mirreh's technicians crafted were necessary to his cause, after the loss of the Great Weapon following Johab's escape. The thought of that Lord, young as he was, filled the man with gloom bordering on despair. Free on the plain of Rehannoth, that youth could wreak unguessable harm on the ambitions of the new lords of the lands.

With grim amusement, Johab saw himself through the mind of his enemy. Even he would have feared an enemy as formidable and mysterious as he was believed to be. But he found with relief that there was no suspicion of his alliance with Ellora—not even, he noted in amusement, the knowledge that Ellora had also escaped. So Mirreh was keeping secrets from his ally . . . a useful thing to know.

Gently he withdrew his seeing from that spirit, glad to be free of its murk and filth. He opened his eyes in the dusty heat beneath the matting, and it felt clean and clear compared with the place where he had been. He hissed between his teeth to let the people know he had returned. They all settled themselves to endure until nightfall.

Slowly the sun moved across the shimmering sky toward the west. The forces of Golath had left the copse long since, but no chance must be taken that the band of plainsfolk might be sighted by them or by abreet sent to meet them. When the tussocks' shadows lay long across the land, the people drew breath more freely. A little coolness found its way beneath the mats, and soon the sun was gone. They climbed from their burrows and hurried again across the plain, bearing their crystals with them.

Greatest caution was now the watchword. One night and then another saw them speeding on their way toward the place of Juthar, where stood the House of Enthala, home of Johab's folk for many generations of their kind. No hum or vibration had been felt from the Great Wheel of Arthoa in all the long journey. It had been kept carefully wrapped and braced. Many of its smaller crystals had been unstrung and carried separately. Yet as they neared Enthala there came a time when those who bore the thing along felt their hair rise on their heads, the skin prickle on their forearms. They called aloud and halted.

Johab came running back along the line of burdened folk, laying aside his own parcel as he stopped by the Wheel.

"Feel it, Lord! It makes us afraid!" cried Thearon. Huthear, his father, nodded shamefacedly and stood aside.

Johab laid his hand upon the thing and felt the potential rising within it. Calling to Jearth and Ruthan, he said, "Lay your hands upon me. Take the bracelet from my arm, Ruthan, as you did before, and focus the light of the triple moons upon my head. Lend me your strength, for I must conquer the Wheel yet again, or it may destroy us all."

Ruthan and Jearth swiftly complied, and Johab slipped his hands beneath the wrappings to lay them on the frame of the Wheel. Closing his eyes, he again exerted his will against the terrible weapon, quenching its vibrations, killing the hum that was building in its heart, subduing all except that eye of undying fire that lay at the heart of the great crystal. When he took away his hands, they were waxen and dead. Ruthan rubbed them with her own until they tingled with life again.

Johab looked about him at the concerned faces of his people. "There is danger here, it is true. But it is only because the thing nears the place that it was made to fill. In its frame upon my father's wall, it is in the magnetic center of Rehannoth. There, the light of sun and moons may fall upon it in such a way that they may be refracted through it, focusing power on any spot toward which it is directed.

"It feels the forces drawing in about it, and its crystals are waking. I have put most of them to sleep again, but we must make haste . . . speed to make all we have done before this look like play. Before the third sunrise, it must be in its place, surrounded by the controls that are built into its frame and the wall."

Without question or delay, the people lifted their burdens and moved across the land, forcing the last reserve of energy from their weary limbs. And such was their determination that in the darkness before the second dawn Johab flung up his hand to halt them.

"There stands Enthala, home of my fathers, built on the place of Juthar. We have come to our journey's end."

Grim in the half-light, the walls stood on the plain, their height made taller yet by the absence of the house that had stood within. The mad light of the triple moons played strange tricks on the gaunt faces of the people, and they stood for a moment in an almost-fear. Then they took up their burdens again and hurried toward that forbidding enclosure, though their hearts felt chill with foreboding long before they came to that dark shelter.

The gates hung upon one riven hinge, and the heavy wood and metal were battered and shattered by the blows that the usurpers had directed against them when they tried to destroy the house of the Plains Lord. The thin breeze of morning whispered about the broken leaves of the gate and the broken stone of the walls. More than one of the folk felt that they heard again the voices of the Old Lords, speaking in their own place. Still, they went inside and stood in that tall circle of stone, feeling the old ashes blow against their cheeks with the sensation of thin fingers stroking.

Johab stood alone, a little apart. His heart was crying out in pain that had come to life again. Here had been the hall where the emblems of all who had gone before had hung. Each had had a plaque describing the accomplishments of its owner. There had been the door to the dining hall, where his father had died between sip and bite, skewered upon the bolt of his own steward. A ragged pile of blackened stone marked the stair down which the henchmen of Golath had dragged him, a child weeping and raging, knowing that his world had ended and never could come again.

Then his mood lightened, as though the whispers on the wind had brought him a message of comfort. From some hidden place in his thought came the image of a butterfly that dipped carelessly into a field of golden flowers.

"The walls of my fathers still stand against the winds," he said fiercely to himself. "The tools with which to right the old wrongs are within our hands. Now is the time for working, not for grief."

He called to Huthear and walked with him to the center of the north wall, which lay at some distance across the rubble-strewn enclosure. They stood beneath the structure, and Johab pointed upward.

"There, where the stone forms an arch over space, as if in ornament, is the place where the Wheel must go. The stairway is set cunningly into the stonework and shows no sign from below. When you find the place where a base stone thrusts out for a foot's width, there is its beginning. Once upon the stair, you cannot fail to see each step that your foot must find next. Up this sheer-seeming height we must bear the Wheel and set it into the metal frame that swivels within that arch. Along the way are hidden projections that fit into slots of the Wheel's own frame, giving its bearers time to rest.

"Now we must eat and rest, for this will be yet another great labor. We have done well, Huthear. Now we must do better."

The plainsman smiled. "We have done the impossible, Lord. Why should we shrink from the merely difficult?"

So they went back and showed the folk where to make fire, that none who walked the plain might know by light or by smoke that the living once again dwelled within the walls of Enthala.

Before the sun topped the wall they slept, but Johab lay waking, seeking for the pulse of life and thought that was Ellora.

15

The Lord Ellora

THERE was blackness shot with streaks of uncertain light; there were rough hands and rougher voices, echoing hollowly. Ellora came slowly to herself, slipping, for a while, back and forth between unconsciousness and alertness.

She felt about her with her seeing sense, at last, finding her capabilities dim and full of effort. Still, she learned that she was being borne along the cavern by men who held light-glasses high to illuminate their way. From him who walked beside her head she received an aura of command, and she slipped into his thought, taking care to make no impression.

Then her senses spun insanely, and her head seemed to swell and collapse about a point of bright-hot pain. Her body moaned, and the thought of the troop leader turned to the sound. Ellora seized the opportunity to retreat into her own skull, painful though that place might presently be. *Something,* she thought, *has damaged me so that I cannot go out into the mind of another.*

For the first time in her long captivity, she felt fear. With the assurance of her mental abilities firmly in her grasp, she was invincible, in her way. Without them . . . without them, could she sustain the bitter role of prisoner again? Could she, more importantly, hold within her heart the secret of Johab's intentions?

She lay now in a darkness of her own, wrestling with despair. The touch of the troopers could not reach her; their voices were inaudible through the tumult of terror that roared through her mind. At the ultimate depth of her agony, she again lost consciousness and did not know that she was being carried swiftly from the dark tunnels to the house of Mirreh.

When she next awoke to her senses, there were again voices. But they were not the rough ones that had pressed in upon her before. No, these were silken voices, used to persuading the simple that sour wine was honey. One of them was hatefully familiar to Ellora, and she lay for a time feigning unconsciousness and gathering her strength. She still made short and futile attempts to send her senses forth from her bruised head, but it was entirely too painful for sustained effort.

When she realized fully that for the present her gift was impaired, she sighed and began to listen and to peer through all-but-closed eyelids.

Mirreh stood with his back to her, arguing in his smooth way with one whom she did not recognize.

"She must return to the deep prison," Mirreh was saying. "She escaped from there, and it is necessary that she be placed there again. Fear is my weapon to hold the people in check, and they must see that the legendary Lord Ellora is only a prisoner, no more."

The tall woman who faced him frowned. Her eyes narrowed, and even from a considerable distance Ellora could see the intelligence that blazed on her generous brow. "Even you, Mirreh, must recognize that it was from that very impregnable hold that she escaped. Recall: you were so terribly shaken when she could not be found anywhere in your domains that you even had me called from the exile you imposed on me. You found that you must, at long last, consult with your mother!

"And when we stood together before the wall where the shackles still hung, locked, upon their chains, you turned to me as though I could mend this happening as I did your infant troubles. What injustice it is that I must bring forth an imbecile!

"I taught you the ways and the needs of power. I gave you the plan that could put it into your hands. And when you found yourself in the place that I had made for you, you turned upon me as though I were a threat. You denied me a place at your side, well-earned though it might be!"

The honeyed voice grew strident, its sweetness lost in bitter emotion. Then the woman calmed, though the effort of will showed clearly on her face and in her bearing. She drew a long breath.

"Still, I am your mother. I have lived long and observed the Lords for many years. I see reality when it burns before my eyes, though seemingly you cannot. So I say to you that you must keep Ellora here in her own chambers and tend her carefully. Speak kindly. Ask no questions . . . yet. She is sorely injured, and it may be that the nature of her injury may cause her to remember little of what has happened in the past. I have seen such things occur with hurts to the head.

"If this should be so, you would have in your hands all the power of the Lords, all the long training, all the secrets, if . . ." and she looked long and hard at her son, "you can persuade her of your gentleness and good faith. If!"

Mirreh twitched his cloak and straightened his shoulders. "If!" He snorted. "You want me to pamper this stubborn woman who has defied and scorned me for years, upon the remote chance that she may not remember the past? If this were so, indeed, why should she remember those precious secrets?"

His mother shrugged. "A sensible man would know that one may accomplish much more with smooth words than with torture, given a subject stronger than himself."

Mirreh jerked as if stung by a whiplash.

". . . And one far more intelligent. If she remembers, you will be no worse off than you were. And if she does not, her training has been of the sort that wears its track into the mind. Her instinct will tell her what we need to know.

"A subtle man, one of wit and perception, would never have hung a young woman upon a dungeon wall for months and years. So I told you before you began that stupid action. You sent me into exile for it. Now I tell you again. And there is another reason. The Lords were loved by the people. You may close your mouth. No matter how you preach the opposite, seeking to hold the obedience of these unspeakable folk you have brought into Olanthe, nevertheless you know and I know that you lie. Even your people know, but the spineless fools cannot remember further back than your last lie.

"Remember, also, that she has been missing from your chains for many, many days. You cannot know where she has been or what she has done—or with whom she has spoken. Perhaps she has accomplices you have never dreamed of. Or perhaps she has made friends in the time since she evaporated from your chains. It is even possible"—and here the woman folded her hands before her and looked down at her fists, her brow furrowed—"that she may have recovered and activated those weapons whose existence you have tried for so long to prove."

Mirreh leaned toward his mother, his narrow face cut into lines of anxiety. "Thassala, this cannot be possible . . . can it? She was found so near the place from which she disappeared . . . surely she merely hid in the caverns and robbed the storehouses to live. She was too weak and ill when she—left—to walk far or to remain alive out in the weather."

Thassala shrugged. "She went as mist from a mirror. You told me that she was in rags when she hung upon your wall. You cannot know where she went, or with whom. Simply think: Now she is clad in a brown garment that looks like the stuff the plainsfolk weave. Now how could she have found such a thing in the storehouses of Olanthe?

"Oh, be sure, Mirreh, she has gone farther than you think and done that which you would not believe. This I know, for I know the Lords. Their powers are strange, unlike those you seek to wring from your puny technicians who must twist wires and mold metal to build silly little engines to power the things they make. The Lords built no engines. They used great wheels of shining stuff for their power. I remember seeing a caravan of such devices being borne through the mountains along the road where I lived as a child. I followed them with the other children of my people until they stopped for the night. When they unwrapped the things they carried, we shivered and ran away. The light of the fires glanced from many gems and burned red and gold and green, with a humming I can remember yet, frightening in its power."

Mirreh's eyes glowed with a light almost as red as that same firelight as he hissed, "Yes! That is what I want. I have questioned that woman for years, seeking some hint of those weapons, but she has laughed and talked nonsense. Many have memories of talk of the Great Wheel of Arthoa. Some few have memories like yours and must have seen it in their youth. Yet no one can say where it was hidden or what it would do. You cannot suppose that she knew . . . all the while . . . That she somehow has reached and set into motion the forces of that terrible thing?"

His mother laughed, a short dry sound that held no mirth. "If it were so, you would likely never know until your time had run past recalling. If she has done what I would have done, given her abilities, you are even now standing upon ruin."

She turned and caught up her cloak from a nearby chair. As she settled it about her shoulders, her son moved close and caught her elbow.

"Thassala, you must stay! You know the Lords as I do not, though I spent years serving Jornaval. You may be able to tame this woman to my purposes . . . and if she has set my ruin in motion, it is to your advantage to learn of it and find how to arrest it. Let us work together in this. I called you from exile because I needed your wisdom. If you aid me, I will be grateful."

The woman's eyes narrowed. For an instant the resemblance between the two was marked, as skepticism and suspicion set their stamps upon her expression. But she relaxed, and the smooth mask of usage slipped again over her features.

"Of course, my son, if you need me I will stay," she purred. "As before, I ask neither power nor wealth, only your trust in my advice. But remember well. If I am sent forth a second time for advising you well against your inclinations, I will not return. Death itself will not sway me."

The two stood, eye to eye, their honeyed voices stilled, their masks fully in place, distrust surrounding them as visibly as fog or smoke. And Ellora, watching through slitted eyes, chose this moment to groan and stir, pretending to awaken.

Thassala was at her side in a moment, laying a cool hand upon her forehead and saying, "Now, my child, you must lie still and not toss about. You have injured your head severely."

Ellora looked up at her, making her eyes wide and bewildered. "Who are you, Lady?" she asked weakly. "What has happened, and why is there a stranger in my chambers? Where is Hamath?" She turned her head restlessly upon the pillow and sighed.

Mirreh drew near and looked down at her. "Do you know me, Ellora?" he asked, and there was a terrible intentness in his gaze.

She let her eyes wander listlessly across his face, nodded, then winced. "You are Mirreh, new-come from the mountains to aid the seneschal in his duties. My father finds you apt . . . but you seem older than I thought." She turned her gaze again to the woman and asked, beseechingly, "Oh, please bring my father to me. I know that he is much occupied with duties, but I would see him."

Thassala took from a nearby table a flask and a cup. "You cannot see him now, child. You must take your medicine and sleep. Then you will be stronger and will learn many things."

Ellora sipped the bitter dose without resistance. She had no fear of attempts upon her life as long as Mirreh sought to learn of the Great Wheel of Arthoa. She had hope that the draught might send her into such deep sleep that she might awaken with her powers healed. So she smiled at the two who stood by the couch, sleepily, sleepily, and allowed her head to droop, her senses to swim away into darkness.

When she woke again, it was to darkness and the knowledge that she had been bathed and wrapped in smooth fabrics. She stretched her legs gratefully against the comfort of fine bed-clothes and felt her spine sinking luxuriously into soft cushionings. She sighed, and a spark of light leaped into being at once.

Thassala, wrapped in a long white bedgown, stood at the foot of the couch.

"Do you require anything, my child?" she asked, her oversweet tone setting Ellora's teeth on edge. "There is food here, if you hunger."

"I am very hungry," said Ellora in the childlike voice that she had settled upon as that most likely to persuade her captors that she truly remembered nothing that had happened since her early youth. "You are kind, Lady. But where is Hamath?"

"I will tell you tomorrow," answered the woman. "Tonight you must eat and rest again. When you are feeling strong and well, then I will answer your questions."

The chilled fowl was good, and the light wine excellent. Ellora finished them neatly and lay back, waving away the cup of medicine. "I will sleep now without help," she said. "Good night, Lady."

When the light was again extinguished, she made her breathing slow and deep. Then she set herself again to find a way into the mind of Thassala. Now there was some response. Her inner self, which had not been trapped inside her own being exclusively since she could remember, moved outward as far as the antechamber where Thassala lay, not sleeping but listening intently to the breathing of the captive. Ellora felt a quiver of amusement. How strange to listen to her own breathing through the ears of another . . . and an enemy!

Gently, carefully, she dipped into the stream that was the woman's thought. It was barely possible, with much pain, for her injured system. Yet there she found the current of ambition that had given direction both to Thassala and her son. With it was a countercurrent of tenderness that might well have been the thing that frustrated her ambitions.

Down into that strange mind went Ellora, probing delicately, ignoring her own agony. The schemes and machinations that had brought Mirreh and his fellow conspirator to power lay bare to her thought, yet they meant nothing to the Lord Ellora in this present state. The one thing she had not deduced already was whatever thing it was in their hearts that had sent them against those who had been their best friends and benefactors.

She had winnowed Mirreh to his roots during her long captivity, finding that he did not understand his own motivations. Now, in his mother, she found them. The deeps of Thassala's heart held a core of bitterness and frustration that left the girl appalled at its cruel pain. Years and generations of suspicion had fueled hatred in a few of the people of Rehannoth, Ellora discovered. Its sole cause, for all she could discern, was the mere existence of the Old Lords.

Bred in the truthfulness and logic of her own people, she

had never conceived of the sort of witches' brew of jealousy and misconstrued motives that existed in this woman's deepest self. She found that no helpful action her folk had ever taken had not been suspect, taken to be a snare, a black plot, aimed at beguiling the ordinary folk of the lands. There was no smooth spot in that troubled spirit whereon the notion of love and aid might perch.

Still weakened as she was, Ellora found herself spun back into her own skull without volition, almost as if there were no place in that other self to hold the cool logic and unemotional interest that made her one of the Lords.

Stunned, she lay in the darkness, examining a new thought, a concept that had never before been entertained by one of her kind. Could it be that by their simple existence the Old Lords had brought into being the instruments of their own downfall? Could it be that their well-intentioned efforts had fostered the bitterness that made such as Mirreh and Thassala . . . and Golath, too, no doubt . . . become what they were?

It was a notion so illogical, so contrary to every tenet of good sense, that the girl almost discarded it. Yet there was a truth in it somewhere. She felt it intuitively. It was almost as if Nature had sought a balance, conjuring up a weight of emotional anti-logic to counterweight the kind of beings the Old Lords had become over the aeons.

Brooding upon that, Ellora sought sleep, but her rest was broken and her dreams unchancy. So caught up was her spirit in that deep mood of doubtfulness that her partly healed senses were closed away to the seeking of Johab, who lay in darkness, seeking desperately for her.

16

The Gray Falcon Stoops

In the heights far to the north and west of Olanthe, Gertra stood in the sunlight and felt her bones shiver with pleasure at being once again in their native place. Below her, hidden by a fold of the stony slopes, lay her village, where the Clan Tarniel lived beneath the whips of the scourgers. Above reared the volute crests and curtains of rock that soared upward toward her grandfather's hidden lair.

For a short moment she enjoyed the sensation of light and freedom that the high places always gave her. Then she turned her face toward the rock and began moving, sometimes inch-wise, sometimes wedge-wise, up them. Her broken arm had healed to an extent in the time of her journey with Ellora. Now it was usable, though she treated it with caution. Thus her speed was greater than a lowlander could comprehend.

Before the orange sun had reached the edge of the western ranges, she stood in the chill and thin-aired ways atop the crest of the Mountain Tarniel. No smoke hung in the air, no faintest trace of any man dwelling nearby was visible on the soil or the rock, but she knew that her grandfather must be within call. Yet she hesitated to break the silence with a cry, so she began to scramble along a cleft that led deeper into the mountaintop. The footing was precarious, for aeons of scree had fallen into the narrow way. She paid little heed to her surroundings until a stone barred her way, and she stooped to find how to move it.

Then she looked up and about, and she found Otor watching her from his seat on another stone deeper in the cleft.

"Granddaughter?" he asked tentatively. "Are you not my Gertra?"

"Truly, Grandfather," she replied, clambering over the stone and hurrying to his side, "I am Gertra, whom you last saw as a lass yet unwed. Since that time much has been done in the world below that would have been better undone. But the sorest word I bring you is the death of my grandmother, who did not long abide your going. It was the pain of her life that her withered limb prevented her coming into the high places with you. She folded herself away in her memories and died soon."

Otor closed his eyes for a moment. Then he opened them and smiled at Gertra. "I knew it would be so," he said. "We had been too long together to go unwounded by parting. None of our folk had thought to tell me, in all these years.

"Now! What brings you here, and with an arm recently broken, if my eyes are not failing me?"

Gertra swayed where she stood. "There is much that you must know . . . and do. But first I must rest and take food. I have come from Olanthe in terrible haste, and few could have bettered my speed. Now I am almost done."

The old man *tchk'd* to himself in reproach. "Come, child, and I'll warm you and feed you. Then we will talk. The wind and the stone want for nothing, and I have lost the way of thinking of the needs of others."

They went deep into the cleft and climbed out by a seemingly impassable chimney to a high spot. There a semicircular wall of rock rose sheer from the mountain, but there was a hidden breach in that wall. Behind it was a pocket of cave, where the old man made his home. It was no rough encampment but a snug retreat, lined with sheepskin hangings to keep out the cold winds and floored with a deep layer of bark from the forests that lay lower down the mountain. His fireplace had been built by the gods, for its flue ran narrow and true, rising straight up through the rock face. His smoke was dispersed so high above that none could detect it, even though he stood just outside his hidden lair.

A small fire simmered on the hearthstone, and Gertra knelt to warm herself while Otor rummaged behind the hangings and came forth with a pair of carven bowls, which he filled from the pot that sat among the coals.

"Why did I make two, I wonder?" he ruminated, shaking his head. "A lonely man's hope for company, I suppose. Now eat, Granddaughter, and gain strength!"

Gertra tasted the steaming stew and looked up in surprise. "This is meat, Grandfather. How can the clan spare meat for you?"

The old man chuckled. "Did you believe that I would live upon this crag as a vulture, taking only leavings? No, child, I learned to snare the small beasts, to find wild growing things, even to hunt the great horned animals of the heights. No longer do I take food from the mouths of my people. I leave game in the sheep pastures for the shepherds to find and carry back to the clan. I have relearned many of the ways of our longfathers who lived in these high places for untold years before the Old Lords tamed the lands about and made our lives more easeful."

Gertra started. "In the old days, Grandfather, before the usurpers came, before I was born, indeed, did you know any of the Old Lords?"

"Jornaval came among his folk often, listening to praise and blame alike, aiding where he could and rebuking where he deemed it needful. Aye, I knew the Lord Jornaval, and even his little daughter, who came with him that she might learn how to rule when he was gone or too old to grapple with governing," Otor answered. "They came like the sun of spring, the Old Lords, into a world of wild and dangerous creatures, and their going left a frost upon the land."

"I have also met with one of them," said Gertra. "That same child you knew, Ellora, is now a woman grown, and she has gone into the caverns below Olanthe to set therein a device for bringing down that lair of wolves. But she has not come forth again from her task, and I fear for her."

Then she told her grandfather of her fall into the rocks and her rescue, and of the journey that came after. "The Lord Johab has spoken, inside my mind, though he lies afar off in the plain. He has set us a task, Grandfather, that may be to your liking. He bids us rally the folk, in secret, that they may be ready when the usurpers fall, and the land is left once more to the wild and dangerous people left leaderless when they go."

Otor leaned forward, his faded eyes glittering in the firelight. "You bring me joy," he said. "Though I may perish together with all of our people, I would die gladly to see the end of the scourgers and their masters. And I am not alone, here in the high places. There are other old gray falcons roosting high on nearby crags.

"Not only those of Tarniel have felt the whips of the scourgers and starved to their tune. Others also have tried to save their people from the bad new ways and have been driven north. To die, they think, those narrow-souled men of the towns. Little do they know of the ways and the abilities of the mountain people!"

Gertra smiled. "The Lords know, Grandfather. Johab stands among the plainsfolk in love and trust, for they are his own. He drew from Ellora the knowledge of her people, those of us who hold true to the old beliefs, however secretly. He loves and trusts us, as well. He wants us to hold our clan ready for the great changes that will soon come."

They talked long, until the east grew pale, delighting in the opportunity. When they went at last to their rest, Gertra lay upon her pile of sheepskins and sought to look out into the long ways, as she had seen Ellora do, communicating with those afar.

The darkness of the cavern lay against her eyelids, seeming to seal them closed, with all the things she wished to send out locked within. For the first time in all her life, she called within the deeps of her spirit to another. That silent voice echoed between the tight-shut walls of her mind, seeming to her to come to nothing.

"Ellora!" she cried. "Ellora!" And the name resounded hollowly round and round the runnels of her heart.

Tears seeped bitterly from the corners of her sealed eyes, and despair wrung her. She knew, by logic and by intuition, that Ellora now lay a prisoner in Olanthe. The thought of that gallant Lord shackled again to a dungeon wall was pain beyond thought. The knowledge that Ellora could have reached her own mind . . . should have done so long before this . . . ate into her heart.

So great was her agony that it lent power beyond her imagining to her sending.

"Ellora!" cried her anguished spirit, and far to the south and east a terribly faint quiver of response flickered into being. At the same moment, she found inside her the voice of Johab, comforting her.

But she paid no heed to his thought. "Listen!" she commanded. "There is an answer, very weak. Listen through my mind, for the Lord Ellora is trying to answer me."

Then the spirit of Johab sharpened to attention, and he focused the power of his seeing and knowing upon the tiny cry that trembled in Gertra's senses. So faint was it that it could carry no words, but they both knew it to be Ellora, and they rejoiced to know that she was still alive.

When the cry stilled, Johab said to Gertra, "As soon as may be, I will search out Olanthe for her with all the power of my spirit. For now, I dare not take the time. The Great Wheel must be set into position and aligned before the dawn that comes beyond the one that soon appears. The position of the moons will be such that it gives utmost power then, and it will not recur for a year. I had hoped that Ellora might return, even with powers impaired, to join with me in our work. Now I only hope that I may have the time to seek her out and warn her to quit the city before I must bring it down.

"Pray for us, Gertra. Petition the gods to strengthen our hands and our spirits, that we may be able to do what must be done."

"Be sure that I will," she replied. "And if it should be, Lord, that you must go into death in the doing, go unafraid. I have come very near, and only good lies at the feet of the gods."

She felt a warmth that was like an unseen smile. "From the place where my father now exists I brought back two things. One was the secret we sought. The other was a certain knowledge that death is only a friend. Farewell, Gertra."

There was a short silence, and she thought that he had gone from her. Then a last whisper moved in her mind. "Know also that you have proved what my people believed . . . that those who are not of the blood of the Lords also possess the gift of inner vision and power. Not only those of the plain, who have used these for long, but also your mountain breed hold the abilities. If it should happen that no Lord is left to guide you, there is that within your own people that will enable you to build again the peaceful ways of living, the joyful pursuits and useful crafts my own kind knew. Take joy in that, Gertra. Again, farewell."

Then he was truly gone. The woman lay on her sheepskins and smiled into the dawnlight. In her mountain-bred bones, the coming of ill weather was apparent; and when the orange sun rose again its face was dim with coming storm.

Otor, bending above his morning cookery, said, "Do not worry overmuch, child. The ways of the Lords are not deterred by cloud and storm. I have seen, in the days of Jornaval, workings with strange instruments whose crystals could glow with power even in the midst of the sheeash. This day will see our own work begun. We will not have time to concern ourselves with the tasks of the Lords. They will attend to their own."

So Gertra curbed her anxiety, comforting herself with the thought that Ellora lived, though the faintness of that cry was a thing to give her pause. When the meal was done, Otor turned to his grandchild and said, "Now you must go down into the sheep pastures and find the shepherd of Tarniel. Bring her to me, and wait in the cleft where you first found me. I must go up, even to the utmost peak, and send abroad a signal to my fellow falcons. They will be mightily heartened, I'll wager, to see it. Today, the falcon stoops, Gertra, though it may be a time before the prey feels our talons."

17

The Great Wheel of Arthoa

THE terrible walls of Enthala rose sheer from the plain that
was the Place of Juthar. Their broken gates were mouths
through which the winds groaned endlessly. Their empty
window sockets seemed to search the lands about for the
enemy who had worked such havoc.

Johab, standing in their shadow, shuddered at his ill fancies
and turned his thought to the Great Wheel that now hung
partway up the wall. Though the sun was not yet risen, the
plainsfolk had been at work for many hours, their task lighted
by the dizzy glow of the triple moons. And now the Wheel began to inch upward again, slowly, span by span. Many anxious
eyes judged its progress, and many apprehensive ears gauged
the anger of its hum.

That hum now rose, a giant insect's war cry, growing in vol-
ume. All motion stopped, and Johab leaped up the all-but-
invisible stair to lay his hands upon the instrument, again
quieting it with his will.

Huthear clambered down to his side. "Before the sun clears
the far wall, Lord, we will have it secured," he said, but his
face was cut by anxious lines.

"We dare not move it in full sunlight," Johab said, "but it
must be in place before tomorrow's dawn, for then the sun and

moons will be aligned for utmost potency. Let us move it again, Huthear, and I will move with it, up the wall, holding it with my spirit."

So it was done. Those who aided and those who witnessed held their breaths and felt the hair rise upon their napes as that terrible Wheel was raised up the wall. The Lord Johab, feeling blindly for the scanty steps, kept his hands upon the central crystal, his eyes closed, his whole being focused upon quelling the thing.

It seemed that life-spans must have passed, but the sun was just topping the farther wall of Enthala when the Wheel reached the top and was thrust, hurriedly now, into its niche. There the rings at the ends of the spokes hooked magically onto a frame set into the stone. The sun struck it fully, before Johab could take away his hands.

Ruthan, from the top of the wall, cried out, "Oh, see! The Lord is wrapped in flame, and I can see the stone behind him! It is an ill omen!"

But Johab stepped away, unhurt, though he seemed dazed. His people helped him down the blind stair and laid him in the shadow of the wall. He struggled to sit, and Ruthan helped him to an easy position. In the deep shade, he still seemed to glow with that orange light that had enwrapped him, and his eyes were set in a painful stare.

Anxiously, his folk attended him, turning their eyes also to the wall, where the swaddled crystals still hummed and buzzed angrily in the growing light. After a time, Johab shuddered and drew a deep breath.

"Ruthan? Huthear? Thearon?" he called. The three came and knelt beside him.

He closed his eyes painfully, then opened them and focused them with careful attention upon his helpers. "Tomorrow will see the working-out of the will of the gods," he said. "With the rising of the sun, the triple moons will stand in the west, and the Wheel will be washed in all the light of power.

Today I must find Ellora, for I need her spirit added to mine in wielding the powers upon which we must call.

"Still, there are many instruments to place in their proper places on the wall, and this I must entrust to you. Each is in a spot below the niche that is to hold it. You all know the care with which they must be raised. All will go upon the wall, with the exception of the rhythyl. You must bring it to me. Go, my children, and complete the work we have begun. I will go afar and find the Lord Ellora."

His eyes closed again, and his companions looked with concern upon his face, which was now lined with more years than even his father could have mustered. All trace of the youth who had come to them from the metal cells was washed away in the fires of effort and power that had engulfed him. Wordlessly, they went to their dangerous work, leaving Johab to his search.

Thus it was that he reached Gertra as she lay in her grandfather's cave. So he found that Ellora was, indeed, still within the walls of Olanthe; not in the dungeons but in the house of Mirreh, which had belonged to Jornaval in older days. Not long was it before Johab found his seeing spirit within that chamber, looking out through the eyes of Ellora, who welcomed him with joy and sadness.

"My dear," she said to him in the silence of her thought, "I am injured. I cannot send out my spirit as before. There is strength returning, but there will be no bringing me forth again from the toils of Mirreh. Yet I can aid you. When you link your spirit with mine, at the appointed hour, I will lend you all that I am, sending along the linkage the power that is mine."

"But Olanthe will be shattered to its roots!" protested Johab. "You will go down in its ruins, and I shall be left alone, the last remnant of the Lords. Is there no way to bring you from Olanthe?"

Ellora smiled, and he felt the strange sadness of that smile strike inward to her heart. "Johab, we are the last. I have been shown . . . by the gods, I do not doubt . . . that we were not saved to begin our old ways again, only to release the people from those who were warped by the jealousy that our kind roused in their spirits. If I perish, or even you, my dearest, it will be the seal of our love upon the work of our people. Not by long lives will we make our handiwork seen by gods and men, but by this short labor, which may send us to join our fathers."

Johab's body, far away at Enthala, shivered convulsively. "You are injured, and strange fancies can accompany such things. It may be that the gods will deliver you from Olanthe . . . and me from the wall of my father's house. It may be that long years and many children are yet to be our portion." But his spirit still shivered, and his words did not convince him.

There was a rattle at the door, and Thassala entered, goblet in hand. Ellora smiled and lifted her fingers in greeting, saying inwardly, "They seek to keep me drugged. They think to keep me in a malleable state for their own purposes. I must pretend to drink, then to sleep. Our way has been made plain, my love. We must work together, when the sun rises tomorrow, for the saving of our people. Let what must be then happen. We will have held true to the ways of our fathers and the gods. Farewell."

Johab opened his eyes, and the walls of Enthala wavered for an instant before seeming firm again. Upon those walls, he could see swaddled shapes in their niches. He sighed and, rising, moved to the foot of the eastern wall and called up to Ruthan, who stood carefully fitting hooks into rings, settling the last of the large weapons into its place.

"Ruthan, you may tell the folk to begin unwrapping the crystals . . . all except the Wheel. That must remain hidden from the light until nightfall. Take care . . . take greatest care. The devices are all dangerous, though none so much as the Great Wheel. Touch lightly, when you touch at all. Move away swiftly, when the task is done. You may begin with the dothal, which stands to your left. Yes, the single diamond shape. Take care!"

Ruthan sidled along the wall until the device was beside her. With cautious fingers, she loosed the strings that bound the wrappings in place, slipped the cloth downward into a bundle and revealed the marvelous crystal. It glowed pink-gold in the westering light, and for a time all within the walls stood in awe, watching the dothal waken to life. Redder glowed the facets at its heart, redder than the light of the sun. The enclosure below was washed in light that seemed tinged with blood. And the Great Wheel of Arthoa, clothed though it was in every protection they could devise, began to hum, softly as nightwind, a forbidding song.

Huthear came to stand beside Johab, watching him anxiously. But Johab smiled at him. "It is time for it to sing, Huthear. Tomorrow it must sing an end to Mirreh and to Golath and to all their little devices that they use to oppress the people of the mountains and the plain. It must sing Olanthe to rubble and Golath's lair to dust. Many things will have an end tomorrow, my friend. May the new world that it brings mean fair and happy lives for the people of Rehannoth."

Now Ruthan moved to the next draped form and began to free it from its wraps. A multi-faceted glitter of small crystals was revealed, sparkling with almost unbearable brightness in the slanting sunlight. As its prisms came to life, a delicate chiming filled the enclosure of Enthala, as the suspended crystals touched and parted and touched again in the growing breeze. The dothal began to hum, a clear tenor note much different from the deep-toned sound of the Wheel.

The plainsfolk now busied themselves with freeing the rest of the crystals. Each new unveiling brought another shower of color and sparkling glints, another treble or bass or clear soprano note to the growing orchestration of sounds and light that had now filled Enthala, rippling up its scarred walls, echoing through its roofless halls and chambers. Never had an entertainment been held in that house that contained so much beauty, so much terror as it now held. Johab, returned to his place against the wall, lay wrapped in such splendor as he had never dreamed could be.

His eyes fixed upon the device of many small crystals, and the voice of Lithial, his father's singer, moved in his memory:

> "See the sasshila
> shiver the firelight
> shimmer the moonlight
> shatter the sunlight
> into a shuddering
> pattern of shardlight,
> glinting with glory,
> glowing with power . . ."

He smiled. From the rippling showers of sparks that wrapped him, from the growing vibration of the walls and the earth that answered those of the crystals would come the final victory of his people. Johab closed his eyes, and he slept.

While he slept, the walls of Enthala thrust themselves against the darkness, pouring upward from their protecting cup a supernal glow that belied the descent of the sun. Those of the plainsfolk who found reason to go out upon the plain found themselves looking upon the most frightening and beautiful vision of their lives. The walls seemed, now, to be permeable to the light within them, as cupped hands about a lamp may show their delicate lacework of vein and bone through the translucent flesh.

But the walls of Enthala were stranger still. For they seemed to shimmer into and out of focus, now there in a star-webbed lattice, now quivered away into the stuff of light itself. The voices of the crystals were pain and joy in the bones, the flesh, the skulls of the people who watched.

Ruthan, called out to see, with Huthear and Thearon, looked with wonder upon the crucible of power that had been a quiet ruin in the Place of Juthar. Then she laid her hand upon her husband's arm. "Jearth, is it my wits wandering, or does the very soil of the plain begin to shimmer with light and to shake with vibration?"

Jearth closed his eyes for a heartbeat, then opened them. He laid his hand, then his ear, then his whole body upon the earth, arms outspread as if to catch every slightest motion. When he stood again, he turned to Huthear, the Eldest of their group.

"The land is beginning to hum, even as does the Great Wheel. There is power at work, Huthear, greater than any we have known or dreamed. The weapon of Golath that destroyed Relah and poisoned the plain was a child's arrow compared with that which the Lord Johab must wield. It is my thought that many of us who stand here may not see tomorrow's dusk. Let us make our songs to the gods while yet we may, for death lies before us."

Huthear bowed his head. "Even so. The Lord Johab gave us warning, and we have gone prayerfully all the days since. Now the time has come to make our spirits ready. All is done that we may do . . . let us go apart and make farewells and speak with the gods."

The triple moons spun their mad pavane, riding up the sky. Morning would find them high in the western span, as they stood only once a year, ready to answer any extraordinary need of the Lords. The land below them, could they have seen it, was dimly lit by their whirl of light. And in one spot a cone of star-white fury blazed, growing in intensity as the hours passed.

Outside the walls, the folk huddled, unable to rest in the

terrible humming glare that was now Enthala. Only Johab lay within, lapped in that insupportable light, sleeping.

On the walls, the crystal-strung weapons seemed to dance in their frames. The Great Wheel, still swaddled, raised its voice to greater and still greater intensity. Yet Johab slept, and no ill dream, no dread premonition disturbed him.

18

The Power of Light and Thought

JOHAB felt the orange sun, though it was still below the horizon. Without looking, he could see the warm outlines shape the ragged eastern edges of the walls of Enthala. He knew in his bones the instant the beam would break over the encircling stone to wash him in its light.

To him, the layer of cloud that overhung the sky did not exist, for he could feel the waxing power of the star as it moved across the plain toward the spot where he lay. The ripple of uneasy wind, the restless feel of the plain that signaled storm to his companions were irrelevant. Only the tempest of light and vibration in which he now existed had reality for him, and it seemed long to the plainsfolk before he appeared at the gate of Enthala to give them their final duty.

"Huthear, Thearon," he said, "you aided in the moving of the Great Wheel from its resting place. Your courage is not to be questioned. Now I ask you to aid me once more, for the love you bear your people and the love we bear toward one another. Help me to unwrap the Wheel of Arthoa. Not your hands but your hearts are my need. Stay me with your steadfastness, that I may not wither away in the flame that will come."

The father looked to the son, and the son nodded. They stepped forward, and Huthear said, "Even into the flame we will follow you, Lord. You bring salvation to all our people."

Then Ruthan stepped forward. "No longer do you have the presence of the Lord Ellora to stand beside you, though I do not doubt that her spirit will be here. Let me go with you, that she may work through me, my hand and my thought. Jearth will stand with us, and we all will strive together."

Johab bowed his head for a moment. Then he turned his face to the people and smiled with such joy and triumph that none who saw ever forgot. "For such reasons the gods have found a way to save you, my children. Such faith and fortitude are too rare to go down into darkness."

The plainsfolk gathered about the five, pleading to be allowed to help, but now Johab was firm. "None who is not needed at the walls must perish," he said. "Take your packs and move away to the mound that rises to the north. There you will see all that passes, but you should be safe, spared to go back to your Elders and to carry on the new lives that are now being molded. Go with our blessings. Go now!"

Without protest, they began to gather their scanty packs together, and soon they were moving across the plain toward the hummock. The storm broke before they reached it, but they paid it no more heed than did Johab. Indeed, the cloud-wrack seemed unable to stop the light of the sun, and even the triple moons shone through it as a pale wash of brightness in the west.

Within the walls of Enthala, there was a strange, rain-whipped, wind-shattered brilliance. As the five climbed the wall to the Wheel, they could see that the stones beneath their feet were glowing from deep within. Their hands seemed almost to sink into the rock of the notches they grasped, so pervasive was the vibration.

The Wheel quivered blindly, seeming to strain at its coverings. When they stood beside it, they felt that they must be invisible, so shaken was every particle of their bodies. Johab stepped near the thing and loosed the bindings, his hands working by instinct alone, for his spirit was questing southward, seeking the Lord Ellora. As the last wrapping fell down the wall, leaving the Wheel to the full power of the hidden sun and the singing instruments that shone along the walls, her spirit made contact. Johab brought it across the miles, cradled it briefly within his heart, and laid his hand on Ruthan's head.

The girl smiled, and the smile became that of Ellora, as she looked out from Ruthan's eyes. "We stand together, my love, as I had not thought to do. All is possible, now. Let us begin!"

Their hands joined, and they turned to face the Wheel. In his right hand, Johab held the rhythyl. He turned it to focus the rainbow spatter of its light full into the heart of the Wheel. The cartwheel-sized crystal shrieked with the impact, shattering the bass-deep hum of the Wheel into multiple and many-toned voices. Across the span of Enthala, the sasshila chimed angrily, the dothal deepened its tone, and all the weapons sang more loudly, more fiercely, until the sound seemed fit to shiver the lands asunder.

Now the two Lords touched the Wheel. Their eyes were set upon it, their hands laid to it, their thoughts arrowed into it, their wills imposed upon it.

Huthear and Thearon, as they had done before, stood mute, enduring, sustaining. Jearth fixed his eyes upon his wife and his will upon her, holding her own spirit steadfast. They heard, in a voice not one could ever after identify surely, words of awful power boom out across the tempest of storm and chiming and light.

"The City of Golath will crumble into ruin, into individual stones, the stones into dust. None who dwell there will come forth save by the will of the gods. All the devices there will shiver away into their native matter, leaving no trace of their designs or workings."

Far to the west, the folk of the city trudged in the wet filth of the streets, labored at their treadmills, carried the unending stream of stone with which their ruler sought to shore up his fortress. Those who thought for themselves had long since been slain or imprisoned or had fled into the plain. It was a city of beasts, some shrewd and self-centered enough to profit from the new regime, most simply beasts of burden.

In the absence of Golath, all moved more slowly than usual. Even the Guards who oversaw the building of walls and fortifications were too depressed by the grim day to crack their long whips about the loins of laggards. Even the children and the dogs lay about under porches and archways, out of the weather, simply enduring their lives.

There was a rumble from the land about, shaking down stones from the walls of Enthala, spreading through the bedrock to shake down stones from the walls of the City of Golath. The plain shivered, and the folk upon the hummock in the Place of Juthar saw it heave like the sea they had only heard tales of. But the folk in the City of Golath knew nothing, ever again, for Golath was fatally near to Enthala, and the full power of the Wheel overtook it and shattered it.

The fires in the crystals ebbed, for a time. The voices quieted a bit. Johab and Ellora leaned against the Wheel, summoning their remaining strength. For a short while there was opportunity to hear the storm, raging now in full fury.

Away to the south, the heaving of the land moved like slow ripples through water. Those who dwelled in Olanthe could not suspect that their ends were upon them, for they were busy with their daily business of cheating and abusing one another. If Golath was a city of beasts of burden, then Olanthe, truly, was one of predators. Mirreh had surrounded himself with his own kind, who tore at one another with fangs made of money or influence.

In the armory of Olanthe, Mirreh and Golath were watching screens that mirrored what was seen by their abased abreet. They observed with disbelief the crumbling of the City of Golath. Their differences forgotten, they turned eye to eye in desperate speculation. Mirreh opened his lips to speak; but before a word could emerge, there came from deep beneath their feet, below the city and the rock of the city, a single terrible note. Inhuman and crystalline, it sang through all the stone.

In that moment, Johab and Ellora again set their wills upon the Wheel, and its irresistible voice moved through the soil and the rock beneath the soil. The lonely crystal sang beneath Olanthe, and when its voice was joined by that of the Wheel, Olanthe was no more.

Through all the vast continent of Rehannoth the note quivered, sounding through the bedrock, even under that all-encompassing ocean. Where the City of Golath and Olanthe had stood, tall clouds of dust towered, to be ripped away by the storm that now lashed the continent from end to end. In the villages on the plain and in the mountains, the people bowed their heads and held fast, their fear turning into hope.

Upon the wall of Enthala, the five stood, ringed with ineffable fires, amid a clamor that was so terrible it was almost silence, the ear being unable to compass it.

Johab raised his hand, and his helpers moved as he motioned them down the wall and away from the ruined house. For one last instant, the eyes of Ellora smiled from the face of Ruthan. Then she was gone, and Ruthan fell into the arms of Jearth, who bore her down the dizzy way, following Huthear and Thearon. As they went, the light grew brighter yet. When Jearth looked back, he saw that the flame was pulsing through Johab, as though he were not of mortal flesh.

When they reached their people at the hummock and turned their faces again to Enthala, they fell to their knees in awe, and many wept. For Johab throbbed upon the wall, larger than any man could be, laced with shards of purest brightness. At his side stood a giant shadow, and those who watched knew it to be Ellora, delaying her journey into the ways of death to stand with him.

The song of the crystals had fused into one tremendous note that rang to the deeps of the planet, setting the very crust beneath the continent and the oceans to cracking. New mountains were sung into being, down the lengths of time, in that music. New continents, undreamed of yet for many generations of men unborn, had their birth there, as the stresses of the universe worked upon the planet's bulk.

There was an uprushing of shattering light; for a moment, Enthala was a castle of the gods, outlined in fire against the forgotten storm-wrack. Then it was gone, with Johab and Ellora, and only a pure pale color spread across the sky.

Into that peaceful shadow flitted two winged shapes, and Ruthan, from the shelter of Jearth's arms, cried, "There are great butterflies in the sky!"

From east to west, in the track of the invisible sun, they flew. Those who watched could see that their wings were the color of blue-white ice, spangled with rubies. Their fragile antennae shone like filaments of silver, and their eyes glinted golden in a thousand facets. They soared high and spiraled downward over the hummock, then went into the west, where the light absorbed them into its fabric.

In the sky, hidden behind the storm-clouds, the triple moons spun madly. In a distant age to come, a comet would divide them, melding two into a large moon and sending the third reeling into isolation. Then two moons would ride the sky over a different kind of world, and no living being would dream that they had been set there by the hands of men.